All Cats Are Gray

Andre Norton

CONTENTS

ALL CATS ARE GRAY

Under normal conditions a whole person has a decided advantage over a handicapped one. But out in deep space the normal may be reversed—for humans at any rate.

Steena of the spaceways—that sounds just like a corny title for one of the Stellar-Vedo spreads. I ought to know, I've tried my hand at writing enough of them. Only this Steena was no glamour babe. She was as colorless as a Lunar plant—even the hair netted down to her skull had a sort of grayish cast and I never saw her but once draped in anything but a shapeless and baggy gray space-all.

Steena was strictly background stuff and that is where she mostly spent her free hours—in the smelly smoky background corners of any stellar-port dive frequented by free spacers. If you really looked for her you could spot her—just sitting there listening to the talk—listening and remembering. She didn't open her own mouth often. But when she did spacers had learned to listen. And the lucky few who heard her rare spoken words—these will never forget Steena.

She drifted from port to port. Being an expert operator on the big calculators she found jobs wherever she cared to stay for a time. And she came to be something like the master-minded machines she tended—smooth, gray, without much personality of her own.

But it was Steena who told Bub Nelson about the Jovan moon-rites—and her warning saved Bub's life six months later. It was Steena who identified the piece of stone Keene Clark was passing around a table one night, rightly calling it unworked Slitite. That started a rush which made ten fortunes overnight for men who were down to their last jets. And, last of all, she cracked the case of the Empress of Mars.

All the boys who had profited by her queer store of knowledge and her photographic memory tried at one time or another to balance the scales. But she wouldn't take so much as a cup of Canal water at their expense, let alone the credits they tried to push on her. Bub Nelson was the only one who got around her refusal. It was he who brought her Bat.

About a year after the Jovan affair he walked into the Free Fall one night and dumped Bat down on her table. Bat looked at Steena and growled. She looked calmly back at him and nodded once. From then on they traveled together—the thin gray woman and the big gray tom-cat. Bat learned to know the inside of more stellar bars than even most spacers visit in their lifetimes. He developed a liking for Vernal juice, drank it neat and quick, right out of a glass. And he was always at home on any table where Steena elected to drop him.

This is really the story of Steena, Bat, Cliff Moran and the Empress of Mars, a story which is already a legend of the spaceways. And it's a damn good story too. I ought to know, having framed the first version of it myself.

For I was there, right in the Rigel Royal, when it all began on the night that Cliff Moran blew in, looking lower than an antman's belly and twice as nasty. He'd had a spell of luck foul enough to twist a man into a slug-snake and we all knew that there was an attachment out for his ship. Cliff had fought his way up from the back courts of Venaport. Lose his ship and he'd slip back there—

to rot. He was at the snarling stage that night when he picked out a table for himself and set out to drink away his troubles.

However, just as the first bottle arrived, so did a visitor. Steena came out of her corner, Bat curled around her shoulders stole-wise, his favorite mode of travel. She crossed over and dropped down without invitation at Cliff's side. That shook him out of his sulks. Because Steena never chose company when she could be alone. If one of the man-stones on Ganymede had come stumping in, it wouldn't have made more of us look out of the corners of our eyes.

She stretched out one long-fingered hand and set aside the bottle he had ordered and said only one thing, "It's about time for the Empress of Mars to appear again."

Cliff scowled and bit his lip. He was tough, tough as jet lining—you have to be granite inside and out to struggle up from Venaport to a ship command. But we could guess what was running through his mind at that moment. The Empress of Mars was just about the biggest prize a spacer could aim for. But in the fifty years she had been following her queer derelict orbit through space many men had tried to bring her in—and none had succeeded.

A pleasure-ship carrying untold wealth, she had been mysteriously abandoned in space by passengers and crew, none of whom had ever been seen or heard of again. At intervals thereafter she had been sighted, even boarded. Those who ventured into her either vanished or returned swiftly without any believable explanation of what they had seen—wanting only to get away from her as quickly as possible. But the man who could bring her in—or even strip her clean in space—that man would win the jackpot.

"All right!" Cliff slammed his fist down on the table. "I'll try even that!"

Steena looked at him, much as she must have looked at Bat the day Bub Nelson brought him to her, and nodded. That was all I saw. The rest of the story came to me in pieces, months later and in another port half the System away.

Cliff took off that night. He was afraid to risk waiting—with a writ out that could pull the ship from under him. And it wasn't until he was in space that he discovered his passengers—Steena and Bat. We'll never know what happened then. I'm betting that Steena made no explanation at all. She wouldn't.

It was the first time she had decided to cash in on her own tip and she was there—that was all. Maybe that point weighed with Cliff, maybe he just didn't care. Anyway the three were together when they sighted the Empress riding, her dead-lights gleaming, a ghost ship in night space.

She must have been an eerie sight because her other lights were on too, in addition to the red warnings at her nose. She seemed alive, a Flying Dutchman of space. Cliff worked his ship skillfully alongside and had no trouble in snapping magnetic lines to her lock. Some minutes later the three of them passed into her. There was still air in her cabins and corridors. Air that bore a faint corrupt taint which set Bat to sniffing greedily and could be picked up even by the less sensitive human nostrils.

Cliff headed straight for the control cabin but Steena and Bat went prowling. Closed doors were a challenge to both of them and Steena opened each as she passed, taking a quick look at what lay within. The fifth door opened on a room which no woman could leave without further investigation.

I don't know who had been housed there when the Empress left port on her last lengthy cruise. Anyone really curious can check back on the old photo-reg cards. But there was a lavish display of silks trailing out of two travel kits on the floor, a dressing table crowded with crystal and jeweled containers, along with other lures for the female which drew Steena in. She was standing in front of the dressing table when she glanced into the mirror—glanced into it and froze.

Over her right shoulder she could see the spider-silk cover on the bed. Right in the middle of that sheer, gossamer expanse was a sparkling heap of gems, the dumped contents of some jewel case. Bat had jumped to the foot of the bed and flattened out as cats will, watching those gems, watching them and—something else!

Steena put out her hand blindly and caught up the nearest bottle. As she unstoppered it she watched the mirrored bed. A gemmed bracelet rose from the pile, rose in the air and tinkled its siren song. It was as if an idle hand played…. Bat spat almost noiselessly. But he did not retreat. Bat had not yet decided his course.

She put down the bottle. Then she did something which perhaps few of the men she had listened to through the years could have done. She moved without hurry or sign of disturbance on a tour about the room. And, although she approached the bed she did not touch the jewels. She could not force herself to that. It took her five minutes to play out her innocence and unconcern. Then it was Bat who decided the issue.

He leaped from the bed and escorted something to the door, remaining a careful distance behind. Then he mewed loudly twice. Steena followed him and opened the door wider.

Bat went straight on down the corridor, as intent as a hound on the warmest of scents. Steena strolled behind him, holding her pace to the unhurried gait of an explorer. What sped before them both was invisible to her but Bat was never baffled by it.

They must have gone into the control cabin almost on the heels of the unseen—if the unseen had heels, which there was good reason to doubt—for Bat crouched just within the doorway and refused to move on. Steena looked down the length of the instrument panels and officers' station-seats to where Cliff Moran worked. On the heavy carpet her boots made no sound and he did not glance up but sat humming through set teeth as he tested the tardy and reluctant responses to buttons which had not been pushed in years.

To human eyes they were alone in the cabin. But Bat still followed a moving something with his gaze. And it was something which he had at last made up his mind to distrust and dislike. For now he took a step or two forward and spat—his loathing made plain by every raised hair along his spine. And in that same moment Steena saw a flicker—a flicker of vague outline against Cliff's hunched shoulders as if the invisible one had crossed the space between them.

But why had it been revealed against Cliff and not against the back of one of the seats or against the panels, the walls of the

6

corridor or the cover of the bed where it had reclined and played with its loot? What could Bat see?

The storehouse memory that had served Steena so well through the years clicked open a half-forgotten door. With one swift motion she tore loose her spaceall and flung the baggy garment across the back of the nearest seat.

Bat was snarling now, emitting the throaty rising cry that was his hunting song. But he was edging back, back toward Steena's feet, shrinking from something he could not fight but which he faced defiantly. If he could draw it after him, past that dangling spaceall…. He had to—it was their only chance.

"What the…." Cliff had come out of his seat and was staring at them.

What he saw must have been weird enough. Steena, bare-armed and shouldered, her usually stiffly-netted hair falling wildly down her back, Steena watching empty space with narrowed eyes and set mouth, calculating a single wild chance. Bat, crouched on his belly, retreating from thin air step by step and wailing like a demon.

"Toss me your blaster." Steena gave the order calmly—as if they still sat at their table in the Rigel Royal.

And as quietly Cliff obeyed. She caught the small weapon out of the air with a steady hand—caught and leveled it.

"Stay just where you are!" she warned. "Back, Bat, bring it back!"

With a last throat-splitting screech of rage and hate, Bat twisted to safety between her boots. She pressed with thumb and forefinger, firing at the spacealls. The material turned to powdery flakes of ash—except for certain bits which still flapped from the scorched seat—as if something had protected them from the force of the blast. Bat sprang straight up in the air with a scream that tore their ears.

"What...?" began Cliff again.

Steena made a warning motion with her left hand. "Wait!"

She was still tense, still watching Bat. The cat dashed madly around the cabin twice, running crazily with white-ringed eyes and flecks of foam on his muzzle. Then he stopped abruptly in the doorway, stopped and looked back over his shoulder for a long silent moment. He sniffed delicately.

Steena and Cliff could smell it too now, a thick oily stench which was not the usual odor left by an exploding blaster-shell.

Bat came back, treading daintily across the carpet, almost on the tips of his paws. He raised his head as he passed Steena and then he went confidently beyond to sniff, to sniff and spit twice at the unburned strips of the spaceall. Having thus paid his respects to the late enemy he sat down calmly and set to washing his fur with deliberation. Steena sighed once and dropped into the navigator's seat.

"Maybe now you'll tell me what in the hell's happened?" Cliff exploded as he took the blaster out of her hand.

"Gray," she said dazedly, "it must have been gray—or I couldn't have seen it like that. I'm colorblind, you see. I can see only shades of gray—my whole world is gray. Like Bat's—his world is gray too—all gray. But he's been compensated for he can see above and below our range of color vibrations and—apparently—so can I!"

Her voice quavered and she raised her chin with a new air Cliff had never seen before—a sort of proud acceptance. She pushed back her wandering hair, but she made no move to imprison it under the heavy net again.

"That is why I saw the thing when it crossed between us. Against your spaceall it was another shade of gray—an outline. So I put out mine and waited for it to show against that—it was our only chance, Cliff.

"It was curious at first, I think, and it knew we couldn't see it—which is why it waited to attack. But when Bat's actions gave it away it moved. So I waited to see that flicker against the spaceall and then I let him have it. It's really very simple...."

Cliff laughed a bit shakily. "But what was this gray thing? I don't get it."

"I think it was what made the Empress a derelict. Something out of space, maybe, or from another world somewhere." She waved her hands. "It's invisible because it's a color beyond our range of sight. It must have stayed in here all these years. And it kills—it must—when its curiosity is satisfied." Swiftly she described the scene in the cabin and the strange behavior of the gem pile which had betrayed the creature to her.

Cliff did not return his blaster to its holder. "Any more of them on board, d'you think?" He didn't look pleased at the prospect.

Steena turned to Bat. He was paying particular attention to the space between two front toes in the process of a complete bath. "I don't think so. But Bat will tell us if there are. He can see them clearly, I believe."

But there weren't any more and two weeks later Cliff, Steena and Bat brought the Empress into the Lunar quarantine station. And that is the end of Steena's story because, as we have been told, happy marriages need no chronicles. And Steena had found someone who knew of her gray world and did not find it too hard to share with her—someone besides Bat. It turned out to be a real love match.

The last time I saw her she was wrapped in a flame-red cloak from the looms of Rigel and wore a fortune in Jovan rubies blazing on her wrists. Cliff was flipping a three-figure credit bill to a waiter. And Bat had a row of Vernal juice glasses set up before him. Just a little family party out on the town.

VOODOO PLANET

I

Talk of heat—or better not—on Xecho. This water-logged world combined all the most unattractive features of a steam bath and one could only dream of coolness, greenness—more land than a stingy string of islands.

The young man on the promontory above the crash of the waves wore the winged cap of a spaceman with the insignia of a cargo-master and not much else, save a pair of very short shorts. He wiped one hand absently across his bare chest and brought it away damp as he studied, through protective sun goggles, the treacherous promise of the bright sea. One could swim—if he wanted to lose most of his skin. There were minute organisms in that liquid that smacked their lips—if they had lips—every time they thought of a Terran.

Dane Thorson licked his own lips, tasting salt, and plodded back through the sand of the spaceport to the berth of the Solar Queen. This had been a long day, and one with more snarl-ups than he cared to count, keeping him on a constant, dogged trot between the ship and the fitting yard where riggers labored with the slowest motions possible to the human body—or so it seemed to the exasperated acting-Cargo-Master of the Free Trader. Captain Jellico had long ago taken refuge in his cabin to preserve the remnants of his temper. Dane had been allowed no such escape.

11

The Queen had a schedule for refitting to serve as a mail ship, and that time allowance did not allow for humidity playing the devil with the innards of robot fitters. She had to be ready to lift when the Combine ship now plying that run set down and formally signed off in her favor. Luckily, most of the work was done and Dane had given a last searching inspection before signing the rigger's book and reporting to his captain.

The air-conditioned interior of the Queen comforted him as he climbed to his quarters. Ship air was flat, chemically pure but unappetizing stuff. Today it was a relief to breathe. Dane went on to the bather. At least there was no lack of water—with the local skinners filtered out. It was chill but relaxing on his gaunt young body.

He was sealing on his lightest tunic when the ramp buzzer sounded. A visitor—oh, not the supervisor-rigger again! Dane went to answer with dragging feet. For the crew of the Queen at the moment numbered exactly four, with himself for general errand boy. Captain Jellico was in his quarters two levels above, Medic Tau was presumably overhauling his supplies, and Sindbad, ship's cat, asleep in some empty cabin.

Dane jerked his tunic into place, very much on his guard as he came to the head of the ramp. But it was not the supervisor-rigger. Dane, thoroughly used to unusual-appearing strangers, both human and alien, was impressed by this visitor.

He was tall, this quiet man, his great height accented by a fit leanness, a narrowness of waist and hip, a length of leg and arm. His main article of clothing was the universal shorts of the Xecho settler. But, being fashioned of saffron yellow, they were the more brilliant because of his darkness of skin. For he was not the warm brown of the Terran Negroes Dane had served beside, though he shared their general features. His flesh was really black, black with an almost bluish sheen. Instead of shirt or tunic, his deep chest was crossed by two wide straps, the big medallion marking their intersection giving forth flashes of gem fire when he breathed. He wore at his belt not the standard stun gun of a spaceman, but a weapon which resembled the more deadly Patrol blaster, as well as a long knife housed in a jeweled and fringed sheath. To the eye he was an example of barbaric force tamed and trimmed to civilized efficiency.

He saluted, palm out, and spoke Galactic Basic with only a suggestion of accent.

"I am Kort Asaki. I believe Captain Jellico expects me."

"Yes, sir!" Dane snapped to attention. So this was the Chief Ranger from fabulous Khatka, Xecho's sister planet.

The other ascended the cat ladder easily, missing no detail of the ship's interior as he passed. His expression was still one of polite interest as his guide rapped on the panel door of Jellico's cabin. And a horrible screech from Queex, the captain's pet hoobat, drowned out any immediate answer. Then followed that automatic thump on the floor of the blue-feathered, crab-parrot-toad's cage, announcing that its master was in residence.

Since the captain's cordial welcome extended only to his guest, Dane regretfully descended to the mess cabin to make unskilled preparations for supper—though there was not much you could do to foul up concentrates in an automatic cooker.

"Company?" Tau sat beyond the cooking unit nursing a mug of

Terran coffee. "And do you have to serve music with the meals, especially that particular selection?"

Dane flushed, stopped whistling in mid-note. "Terra Bound" was old and pretty well worn out; he didn't know why he always unconsciously sounded off with that.

"A Chief Ranger from Khatka just came on board," he reported, carefully offhand, as he busied himself reading labels. He knew better than to serve fish or any of its derivatives in disguise again.

"Khatka!" Tau sat up straighter. "Now there's a planet worth visiting."

"Not on a Free Trader's pay," commented Dane.

"You can always hope to make a big strike, boy. But what I wouldn't give to lift ship for there!"

"Why? You're no hunter. How come you want to heat jets for that port?"

"Oh, I don't care about the game preserves, though they're worth seeing, too. It's the people themselves—"

"But they're Terran settlers, or at least from Terran stock, aren't they?"

"Sure," Tau sipped his coffee slowly. "But there are settlers and settlers, son. And a lot depends upon when they left Terra and why, and who they were—also what happened to them after they landed out here."

"And Khatkans are really special?"

14

"Well, they have an amazing history. The colony was founded by escaped prisoners—and just one racial stock. They took off from Earth close to the end of the Second Atomic War. That was a race war, remember? Which made it doubly ugly." Tau's mouth twisted in disgust. "As if the color of a man's skin makes any difference in what lies under it! One side in that line-up tried to take over Africa—herded most of the natives into a giant concentration camp and practiced genocide on a grand scale. Then they were cracked themselves, hard and heavy. During the confusion some survivors in the camp staged a revolt, helped by the enemy. They captured an experimental station hidden in the center of the camp and made a break into space in two ships which had been built there. That voyage must have been a nightmare, but they were desperate. Somehow they made it out here to the rim and set down on Khatka without power enough to take off again—and by then most of them were dead.

"But we humans, no matter what our race, are a tough breed. The refugees discovered that climatically their new world was not too different from Africa, a lucky chance which might happen only once in a thousand times. So they thrived, the handful who survived. But the white technicians they had kidnaped to run the ships didn't. For they set up a color bar in reverse. The lighter your skin, the lower you were in the social scale. By that kind of selective breeding the present Khatkans are very dark indeed.

"They reverted to the primitive for survival. Then, about two hundred years ago, long before the first Survey Scout discovered them, something happened. Either the parent race mutated, or, as sometimes occurs, a line of people of superior gifts emerged—not in a few isolated births, but with surprising regularity in five

15

family clans. There was a short period of power struggle until they realized the foolishness of civil war and formed an oligarchy, heading a loose tribal organization. With the Five Families to push and lead, a new civilization developed, and when Survey came to call they were no longer savages. Combine bought the trade rights about seventy-five years ago. Then the Company and the Five Families got together and marketed a luxury item to the galaxy. You know how every super-jet big shot on twenty-five planets wants to say he's hunted on Khatka. And if he can point out a graz head on his wall, or wear a tail bracelet, he's able to strut with the best. To holiday on Khatka is both fabulous and fashionable—and very, very profitable for the natives and for Combine who sells transportation to the travelers."

"I hear they have poachers, too," Dane remarked.

"Yes, that naturally follows. You know what a glam skin brings on the market. Wherever you have a rigidly controlled export you're going to have poachers and smugglers. But the Patrol doesn't go to Khatka. The natives handle their own criminals. Personally, I'd cheerfully take a ninety-nine-year sentence in the Lunar mines in place of what the Khatkans dish out to a poacher they net!"

"So that rumor has spread satisfactorily!"

Coffee slopped over the brim of Tau's mug and Dane dropped the packet of steak concentrate he was about to feed into the cooker. Chief Ranger Asaki loomed in the doorway of the mess as suddenly as if he had been teleported to that point.

The medic arose to his feet and smiled politely at the visitor.

"Do I detect in that observation, sir, the suggestion that the tales I have heard were deliberately set to blast where they would do the most good as deterrents?"

A fleeting grin broke the impassive somberness of the black face.

"I was informed you are a man skilled in 'magic,' Medic. You certainly display the traditional sorcerer's quickness of wit. But this rumor is also truth." The quirk of good humor had gone again, and there was an edge in the Chief Ranger's voice which cut. "Poachers on Khatka would welcome the Patrol in place of the attention they now receive."

He came into the mess cabin, Jellico behind him, and Dane pulled down two of the snap seats. He was holding a mug under the spout of the coffee dispenser as the captain made introductions.

"Thorson—our acting-cargo-master."

"Thorson," the Khatkan acknowledged with a grave nod of his head, and then glanced down to floor level with a look of surprise. Weaving a pattern about his legs, purring loudly, Sindbad was offering an unusually fervent welcome of his own. The Ranger went down on one knee, his hand out for Sindbad's inquiring sniff. Then the cat butted that dark palm, batted at it playfully with claw-sheathed paw.

"A Terran cat! It is of the lion family?"

"Far removed," Jellico supplied. "You'd have to add a lot of bulk to Sindbad to promote him to the lion class."

"We have only the old tales." Asaki sounded almost wistful as the cat jumped to his knee and clawed for a hold on his chest belts. "But I do not believe that lions were ever so friendly toward my ancestors."

Dane would have removed the cat, but the Khatkan arose with Sindbad, still purring loudly, resting in the crook of his arm. The Ranger was smiling with a gentleness which changed the whole arrogant cast of his countenance.

"Do not bring this one to Khatka with you, Captain, or you will never take him away again. Those who dwell in the inner courts would not let him vanish from their sight. Ah, so this pleases you, small lion?" He rubbed Sindbad gently under the throat and the cat stretched his neck, his yellow eyes half closed in bliss.

"Thorson," the Captain turned to Dane, "that arrival report on my desk was the final one from Combine?"

"Yes, sir. There's no hope of the Rover setting down here before that date."

Asaki sat down, still holding the cat. "So you see, Captain, fortune has arranged it all. You have two tens of days. Four days to go in my cruiser, four days for your return here, and the rest to explore the preserve. We could not ask for better luck, for I do not know when our paths may cross again. In the normal course of events I will not have another mission to Xecho for a year, perhaps longer. Also—" He hesitated and then spoke to Tau. "Medic, Captain Jellico has informed me that you have made a study of magic on many worlds."

"That is so, sir."

"Do you then believe that it is real force, or that it is only a superstition for child-people who set up demons to howl petitions to when some darkness falls upon them?"

"Some of the magic I have seen is trickery, some of it founded

18

upon an inner knowledge of men and their ways which a shrewd witch doctor can use to his advantage. There always remains"— Tau put down his mug, "—there always remains a small residue of happenings and results for which we have not yet found any logical explanations—"

"And I believe," Asaki interrupted, "it is also true that a race can be conditioned from birth to be sensitive to forms of magic so that men of that blood are particularly susceptible." That was more of a statement than a question, but Tau answered it.

"That is very true. A Lamorian, for example, can be 'sung' to death. I have witnessed such a case. But upon a Terran or another off-world man the same suggestion would have no effect."

"Those who settled Khatka brought such magic with them." The Chief Ranger's fingers still moved about Sindbad's jaw and throat soothingly, but his tone was chill, the coldest thing in the cramped space of the mess cabin.

"Yes, a highly developed form of it," Tau agreed.

"More highly developed perhaps than even you can believe, Medic!" That came in a hiss of cold rage. "I think that its present manifestation—death by a beast that is not a beast—could be worth your detailed study."

"Why?" Tau came bluntly to the point.

"Because it is a killing magic and it is being carefully used to rid my world of key men, men we need badly. If there is a weak point in this cloudy attack shaping against us, we must learn it, and soon!"

It was Jellico who added the rest. "We are invited to visit Khatka and survey a new hunting range as Chief Ranger Asaki's personal term guests."

Dane drew a deep breath of wonder. Guest rights on Khatka were jealously guarded—they were too valuable to their owners to waste. Whole families lived on the income from the yearly rental of even half a one. But the Rangers, by right of office, had several which they could grant to visiting scientists or men from other worlds holding positions similar to their own. To have such an opportunity offered to an ordinary Trader was almost incredible.

His wonder was matched by Tau's and must have been plain to read for the Chief Ranger smiled.

"For a long time Captain Jellico and I have exchanged biological data on alien life-forms—his skill in photographing such, his knowledge as an xenobiologist are widely recognized. And so I have permission for him to visit the new Zoboru preserve, not yet officially opened. And you, Medic Tau, your help, or at least your diagnosis, we need in another direction. So, one expert comes openly, another not so openly. Though, Medic, your task is approved by my superiors. And"—he glanced at Dane—"perhaps to muddle the trail for the suspicious, shall we not ask this young man also?"

Dane's eyes went to the captain. Jellico was always fair and his crew would have snapped into action on his word alone—even if they were fronting a rain of Thorkian death darts and that order was to advance. But, on the other hand, Dane would never have asked a favor, and the best he hoped for was to be able to perform his duties without unfavorable comment upon their commission. He had no reason to believe Jellico was willing to agree to this.

"You have two weeks' planet-side leave coming, Thorson. If you want to spend it on Khatka...." Jellico actually grinned then. "I take it that you do. When do we up-ship, sir?"

"You said that you must wait for the return of your other crew members—shall we say mid-afternoon tomorrow?" The Chief Ranger stood up and put Sindbad down though the cat protested with several sharp meows.

"Small lion," the tall Khatkan spoke to the cat as to an equal, "this is your jungle, and mine lies elsewhere. But should you ever grow tired of traveling the stars, there is always a home for you in my courts."

When the Chief Ranger went out the door, Sindbad did not try to follow, but he uttered one mournful little cry of protest and loss.

"So he wants a trouble shooter, does he?" Tau asked. "All right, I'll try to hunt out his goblins for him; it'll be worth that to visit Khatka!"

Dane, remembering the hot glare of the Xecho spaceport, the sea one could not swim in, contrasted that with the tri-dees he had seen of the green hunters' paradise on the next planet of the system. "Yes, sir!" he echoed and made a haphazard choice for the cooker.

"Don't be too lighthearted," Tau warned. "I'll say that any stew which was too hot for that Ranger to handle might give us burned fingers—and quick. When we land on Khatka, walk softly and look over your shoulder, and be prepared for the worst."

II

Lightning played along the black ridges above them, and below was a sheer drop to a river which was only a silver thread. Under their boots, man-made and yet dominating the wildness of jungle and mountain, was a platform of rock slabs, fused to support a palace of towering yellow-white walls and curved cups of domes, a palace which was also half fortress, half frontier post.

Dane set his hands on the parapet of the river drop, blinked as a lightning bolt crackled in a sky-splitting glare of violet fire. This was about as far from the steaming islands of Xecho as a man could imagine.

"The demon graz prepare for battle." Asaki nodded toward the distant crackling.

Captain Jellico laughed. "Supposed to be whetting their tusks, eh? I wouldn't care to meet a graz that could produce such a display by mere tusk whetting."

"No? But think of the reward for the tracker who discovers where such go to die. To find the graveyard of the graz herds would make any man wealthy beyond dreams."

"How much truth is there in that legend?" Tau asked.

The Chief Ranger shrugged. "Who can say? This much is true: I have served my life in the forests since I could walk. I have listened to the talk of Trackers, Hunters, Rangers in my father's courtyards and field camps since I could understand their words. Yet never has any man reported the finding of a body of a graz that died a natural death. The scavengers might well account for the bulk of flesh, but the tusks and the bones should be visible for years. And this, too, I have seen with my own eyes: a graz close to death, supported by two of its kind and being urged along to the big swamps. Perhaps it is only that the suffering animal longs for water at its end, or perhaps in the heart of that morass there does lie the graz graveyard. But no man has found a naturally dead graz, nor has any returned from exploring the big swamps...."

Lightning on peaks which were like polished jet—bare rock above, the lush overgrowth of jungle below. And between, this fortress held by men who dared both the heights and the depths. The wildly burgeoning life of Khatka had surrounded the off-worlders since they had come here. There was something untameable about Khatka; the lush planet lured and yet repelled at the same time.

"Zoboru far from here?"

The Chief Ranger pointed north in answer to the captain's question.

"About a hundred leagues. It is the first new preserve we have prepared in ten years. And it is our desire to make it the best for tri-dee hunters. That is why we are now operating taming teams–"

"Taming teams?" Dane had to ask.

The Chief Ranger was ready enough to discuss his project.

"Zoboru is a no-kill preserve. The animals, they come to learn that after a while. But we cannot wait several years until they do. So we make them gifts." He laughed, evidently recalling some incident. "Sometimes, perhaps, we are too eager. Most of our visitors who wish to make tri-dees want to picture big game—graz, amplet, rock apes, lions—"

"Lions?" echoed Dane.

"Not Terran lions, no. But my people, when they landed on Khatka, found a few animals that reminded them of those they had always known. So they gave those the same names. A Khatkan lion is furred, it is a hunter and a great fighter, but it is not the cat of Terra. However, it is in great demand as a tri-dee actor. So we summon it out of lurking by providing free meals. One shoots a poli, a water rat, or a landeer and drags the carcass behind a low-flying flitter. The lion springs upon the moving meat, which it can also scent, and the rope is cut, leaving a free dinner.

"The lions are not stupid. In a very short time they connect the sound of a flitter cutting the air with food. So they come to the banquet and those on the flitter can take their tri-dee shots at ease. Only there must also be care taken in such training. One forest guard on the Komog preserve became too enterprising. He dragged his kill at first. Then, to see if he could get the lions to forget man's presence entirely, he hung the training carcasses on the flitter, encouraging them to jump for their food.

"For the guard that was safe enough, but it worked too too well. A month or so later a Hunter was escorting a client through Komog and they swung low to get a good picture of a water rat emerging from the river. Suddenly there was a snarl behind them and they found themselves sharing the flitter with a lioness annoyed at finding no meat waiting on board.

"Luckily, they both wore stass belts; but they had to land the flitter and leave until the lioness wandered off, and she seriously damaged the machine in her irritation. So now our guards play no more fancy tricks while on taming runs. Tomorrow—no," he corrected himself, "the day after tomorrow I will be able to show you how the process works."

"And tomorrow?" inquired the captain.

"Tomorrow my men make hunting magic." Asaki's voice was expressionless.

"Your chief witch doctor being?" questioned Tau.

"Lumbrilo." The Chief Ranger did not appear disposed to add to that but Tau pursued the subject.

"His office is hereditary?"

"Yes. Does that make any difference?" For the first time there was a current of repressed eagerness in the other's tone.

"Perhaps a vast amount of difference," Tau replied. "A hereditary office may carry with it two forms of conditioning, one to influence its holder, one to affect the public-at-large. Your Lumbrilo may have come to believe deeply in his own powers; he would be a very remarkable man if he did not. It is almost certain that your people unquestionably accept him as a worker of wonders?"

"They do so accept." Once more Asaki's voice was drained of life.

"And Lumbrilo does not accept something you believe necessary?"

"Again the truth, Medic. Lumbrilo does not accept his proper place in the scheme of things!"

"He is a member of one of your Five Families?"

"No, his clan is small, always set apart. From the beginning here, those who spoke for gods and demons did not also order men."

"Separation of church and state," commented Tau thoughtfully. "Yet in our Terran past there have been times when church and state were one. Does Lumbrilo desire that?"

Asaki raised his eyes to the mountain peaks, to the northward where lay his beloved work.

"I do not know what Lumbrilo wants, save that it makes mischief—or worse! This I tell you: hunting magic is part of our lives and it has at its core some of those unexplainable happenings which you have acknowledged do exist. I have used powers I can neither explain nor understand as part of my work. In the jungle and on the grasslands an off-worlder must guard his life with a stass belt if he goes unarmed. But I—any of my men—can walk unharmed if we obey the rules of our magic. Only Lumbrilo does other things which his forefathers did not. And he boasts that he can do more. So he has a growing following of those who believe—and those who fear."

"You want me to face him?"

The Chief Ranger's big hands closed upon the rim of the parapet as if they could exert enough pressure to crumble the hard stone. "I want you to see whether there is trickery in this. Trickery I can fight, for that there are weapons. But if Lumbrilo truly controls forces for which there is no name, then perhaps we must patch up an uneasy peace—or go down in defeat. And, off-worlder, I come from a line of warriors—we do not drink defeat easily!"

"That I also believe," Tau returned quietly. "Be sure, sir, if there is trickery in this man's magic and I can detect it, the secret shall be yours."

"Let us hope that so it shall be."

Subconsciously, Dane had always associated the practice of magic with darkness and the night. But the next morning the sun was high and hot when he made one of the party coming down to a second and larger walled terrace where the Hunters, Trackers, Guards and other followers of the Chief Ranger were assembled in irregular rows.

There was a low sound which was more a throb in the clear air about them, getting into a man's blood and pumping in rhythm there. Dane tracked the sound to its source: four large drums standing waist high before the men who tapped them delicately with the tips of all ten fingers.

The necklaces of claws and teeth about those dusky throats, the kilts of fringed hide, the crossed belts of brilliantly spotted or striped fur were in contrast to the very efficient and modern side arms each man wore, to the rest of the equipment sheathed and strapped at their belts.

There was a carved stool for the Chief Ranger, another for Captain Jellico. Dane and Tau settled themselves on the less comfortable seats of the terrace steps. Those tapping fingers increased their rate of beat, and the notes of the drums rose from the low murmur of hived bees to the mutter of mountain thunder still half a range away. A bird called from those inner courts of the palace from which the women never ventured.

Da—da—da—da.... Voices took up the thud-thud of the drums, the heads of the squatting men moved in a slow swing from side to side. Tau's hand closed about Dane's wrist and the younger man looked around, startled, to see that the medic's eyes were alight, that he was watching the assembly with the alertness of Sindbad approaching prey.

"Calculate the stowage space in Number One hold!"

That amazing order, delivered in a whisper, shocked Dane into obeying it. Number One hold ... there were three divisions now and the stowage was—He became aware that for a small space of time he had escaped the net being woven by the beat of the drum, the drone of voices, the nodding of heads. He moistened his lips. So that was how it worked! He had heard Tau speak often enough about self-hypnotism under such conditions, but this was the first time the meaning of it had been clear.

Two men were shuffling out of nowhere, wearing nothing on their dark bodies but calf-length kilts of tails, black tails with fluffy white tips, which swayed uniformly in time to their pacing feet. Their heads and shoulders were masked by beautifully cured and semi-mounted animal heads displaying half-open jaws with double pairs of curved fangs. The black-and-white striped fur, the sharply pointed ears, were neither canine nor feline, but a weird combination of the two.

Dane gabbled two trading formulas under his breath and tried to think of the relation of Samantine rock coinage to galactic credits. Only this time his defenses did not work. From between the two shuffling dancers padded something on four feet. The canine-feline creature was more than just a head; it was a loose-limbed, graceful body fully eight feet in length, and the red eyes in the prick-eared head were those of a confident killer. It walked without restraint, lazily, with arrogance, its white-tufted tail swinging. And when it reached the mid-point of the terrace, it flung up its head as if to challenge. But words issued from between those curved fangs, words which Dane might not understand but which undoubtedly held meaning for the men nodding in time to the hypnotic cadence of that da — da — da....

"Beautiful!" Tau spoke in honest admiration, his own eyes almost as feral as those of the talking beast as he leaned forward, his fists on his knees.

Now the animal was dancing also, its paws following the pace set by the masked attendants. It must be a man in an animal skin. But Dane could hardly believe that. The illusion was too perfect. His own hands went to the knife sheath at his belt. Out of deference to local custom they had left their stun rods in the palace, but a belt knife was an accepted article of apparel. Dane slid the blade out surreptitiously, setting its point against the palm of his hand and jabbing painfully. This was another of Tau's answers for breaking a spell. But the white and black creature continued to dance; there was no blurring of its body lines into those of a human being.

It sang on in a high-pitched voice, and Dane noted that those of the audience nearest the stools where Asaki and the captain were seated now watched the Chief Ranger and the space officer. He felt Tau tense beside him.

"Trouble coming...." The warning from Tau was the merest thread of sound. Dane forced himself to look away from the swaying cat-dog, to watch instead the singers who were now furtively eying their lord and his guest. The Terran knew that there were feudal bonds between the Ranger and his men. But suppose this was a showdown between Lumbrilo and Asaki—whose side would these men take?

He watched Captain Jellico's hand slide across his knee, his fingers drop in touching distance of knife hilt. And the hand of the Chief Ranger, hanging lax at his side, suddenly balled into a fist.

"So!" Tau expelled the word as a hiss. He moved with sure-footed speed. Now he passed between the stools to confront the dancing cat-dog. Yet he did not look at that weird creature and its attendants. Instead his arms were flung high as if to ward off—or perhaps welcome—something on the mountain side as he shouted:

"Hodi, eldama! Hodi!"

As one, those on the terrace turned, looked up toward the slope. Dane was on his feet, holding his knife as he might a sword. Though of what use its puny length would be against that huge bulk moving in slow majesty toward them, he did not try to think.

Gray-dark trunk curled upward between great ivory tusks, ears went wide as ponderous feet crunched volcanic soil. Tau moved forward, his hands still upraised, clearly in greeting. That trunk touched skyward as if in salute to the man who could be crushed under one foot.

"Hodi, eldama!" For the second time Tau hailed the monster elephant and the trunk raised in silent greeting from one lord of an earth to another he recognized as an equal. Perhaps it had been a thousand years since man and elephant had stood so, and then there had been only war and death between them. Now there was peace and a current of power flowing from one to the other. Dane sensed this, saw the men on the terrace likewise drawing back from the unseen tie between the medic and the bull he had so clearly summoned.

Then Tau's upheld hands came together in a sharp clap and men held their breath in wonder. Where the great bull had stood there was nothing—except rocks in the sun.

As Tau swung around to face the cat-dog, that creature had no substance either. For he fronted no animal but a man, a small, lean man whose lips wrinkled back from his teeth in a snarl. His attendant priests fell back, leaving the spaceman and the witch doctor alone.

"Lumbrilo's magic is great," Tau said evenly. "I hail Lumbrilo of Khatka." His hand made the open-palmed salute of peace.

The snarl faded as the man brought his face under control. He stood naked, but he was clothed in inherit dignity. And there was power with that dignity, power and a pride before which even the more physically impressive Chief Ranger might have to give place.

"You have magic also, outlander," he replied. "Where walks this long-toothed shadow of yours now?"

"Where once the men of Khatka walked, Lumbrilo. For it was men of your blood who long, long past hunted this shadow of mine and made its body their prey."

"So that it now might have a blood debt to settle with us, outlander?"

"That you said, not I, man of power. You have shown us one

31

beast, I have shown another. Who can say which of them is stronger when it issues forth from the shadows?"

Lumbrilo pattered forward, his bare feet making little sound on the stones of the terrace. Now he was only an arm's-length away from the medic.

"You have challenged me, off-world man." Was that a question or a statement? Dane wondered.

"Why should I challenge you, Lumbrilo? To each race its own magic. I come not to offer battle." His eyes held steady with the Khatkan's.

"You have challenged me." Lumbrilo turned away and then looked back over his shoulder. "The strength you depend upon may become a broken staff, off-worlder. Remember my words in the time when shadows become substance, and substance the thinnest of shadows!"

III

"You are truly a man of power!"

Tau shook his head in answer to that outburst from Asaki.

"Not so, sir. Your Lumbrilo is a man of power. I drew upon his power and you saw the results."

"Deny it not! What we saw never walked this world."

Tau slung the strap of a trail bag over his shoulder. "Sir, once men of your blood, men who bred your race, hunted the elephant. They took his tusks for their treasure, feasted upon his flesh—yes, and died beneath the trampling of his feet when they were unlucky or unwary. So there is that within you which can even now be awakened to remember eldama in his might when he was king of the herd and need fear nothing save the spears and cunning of small, weak men. Lumbrilo had already awakened your minds to see what he willed you to see."

"How does he do this?" asked the other simply. "Is it magic that we see not Lumbrilo but a lion before us?"

"He weaves his spell with the drums, with the chant, by the suggestion his mind imposes upon yours. And, having woven his spell, he cannot limit it to just the picture he suggests if ancient racial memories raise another. I merely used the tools of Lumbrilo to show you yet another picture your people once knew well."

"And in so doing made an enemy." Asaki stood before a rack of very modern weapons. Now he made his selection, a silver tube with a stock curved to fit a man's shoulder. "Lumbrilo will not forget."

Tau laughed shortly. "No, but then I have merely done as you wished, have I not, sir? I have focused on myself the enmity of a dangerous man, and now you hope I shall be forced, in self-defense, to remove him from your path."

The Khatkan turned slowly, resting the weapon across his forearm. "I do not deny that, spaceman."

"Then matters here are indeed serious—"

"They are so serious," Asaki interrupted, speaking not only to Tau but to the other off-worlders as well, "that what happens now may mean the end of the Khatka that I know. Lumbrilo is the most dangerous game I have faced in a lifetime as a hunter. He goes, or we draw his fangs—or else all that I am, all I have labored here to build, will be swept away. To preserve this I will use any weapon."

"And I am now your weapon, which you hope will be as successful as that needler you are carrying." Tau laughed again, without much humor. "Let us hope I shall prove as effective."

Jellico moved out of the shadows. It was just after dawn, and the grayness of the vanishing night still held in the corners of the armory. Deliberately he took his own stand before the arms racks and chose a short-barreled blaster. Only when its butt was cupped in his hand did he glance at his host.

"We came guesting, Asaki. We have eaten salt and bread under this roof."

"On my body and my blood it is," returned the Khatkan grimly. "I shall go down to the blackness of Sabra before you do, if the flames of death are against us." From his belt he flipped loose his knife and offered the hilt to Jellico. "My body for a wall between you and the dark, Captain. But also understand this: to me, what I do now is greater than the life of any one man. Lumbrilo and the evil behind him must be rooted out. There was no trickery in my invitation!"

They stood eye to eye, equal in height, in authority of person, and that indefinable something which made them both masters in their own different worlds. Then Jellico's hand went out, his fingertip flicked the hilt of the bared blade.

"There was no trickery," he conceded. "I knew that your need was great when you came to the Queen."

Since both the captain and Tau appeared to accept the situation, Dane, not quite understanding it all, was prepared to follow their lead. And for the moment they had nothing more in plan than to visit the Zoboru preserve.

They went by flitter—Asaki, one of his Hunter pilots, and the three from the Queen—lifting over the rim of mountains behind the fortress-palace and speeding north with the rising sun a flaming ball to the east. Below, the country was stark—rocks and peaks, deep purple shadows marking the veins of crevices. But that was swiftly behind and they were over a sea of greens, many shades of green, with yellow, blue, even red cutting into the general verdant carpet of treetops. Another chain of heights and then open land, swales of tall grass already burnt yellow by the steady sun. There was a river here, a crazy, twisted stream coiling nearly back upon itself at times.

Once more broken land, land so ravished by prehistoric volcanic action that it was a grotesque nightmare of erosion-whittled outcrops and mesas. Asaki pointed to the east. There was a dark patch widening out into a vast wedge.

"The swamp of Mygra. It has not yet been explored."

"You could air map it," Tau began.

The Chief Ranger was frowning. "Four flitters have been lost trying that. Com reports fail when they cross that last mountain ridge eastward. There is some sort of interference which we do not yet understand. Mygra is a place of death; later we may be able to travel along its fringe and then you shall see. Now—" He spoke to the pilot in his own tongue and the flitter pointed up-nose at an angle as they climbed over the highest peak they had yet seen in this mountainous land, to reach at last a country of open grass dotted with small forest stands. Jellico nodded approvingly.

"Zoboru?"

"Zoboru," Asaki assented. "We shall go up to the northern end of the preserve. I wish to show you the roosts of the fastals. This is their nesting season and the sight is one you will long remember. But we shall take an eastern course; I have two Ranger stations to check on the way."

It was after they left the second station that the flitter swung farther out eastward, again climbing over the chain of heights to sight one of the newly discovered wonders the staff at the last station had reported—a crater lake.

And the flitter skimmed down across water which was a rich

emerald in hue, filling the crater from one rock wall to the other with no beach at the foot of those precipitant cliffs. As the machine arose to clear the far wall, Dane tensed. One of his duties aboard the Queen was flitter pilot for planetwise trips. And ever since they had taken off that morning he had unconsciously flown with the Khatkan pilot, anticipating each change or adjustment of the controls. Now he felt that sluggish response to the other's lift signal, and instinctively his own hand went out to adjust a power feed lever.

They made the rise, were well above the danger of the cliff wall. But the machine was not responding properly. Dane did not need to watch the pilot's swiftly moving hands to guess that they were in trouble. And his slight concern deepened into something else as the flitter began to drop nose again. In front of him, Captain Jellico shifted uneasily, and Dane knew that he, too, was alerted.

Now the pilot had plunged the power adjuster to the head against the control board. But the nose of the flitter acted as if it were overweighted or magnetically attracted by the rocks below. The best efforts of the man flying it could not keep it level. They were being drawn earthward, and all the pilot could do only delayed the inevitable crack-up. The Khatkan was turning the machine north to avoid what lay below, for here a long arm of the Mygra swamp clasped about the foot of the mountain.

The Chief Ranger spoke into the mike of the com unit while the pilot continued to fight against the pull which was bringing them down. Now the small machine was below the level of the volcanic peak which cradled the lake, and the mountain lay between them and the preserve.

Asaki gave a muffled exclamation, slapped the com box, spoke more sharply into the mike. It was apparent he was not getting the results he wanted. Then with a quick glance about he snapped an order:

"Strap in!"

His Terran companions had already buckled the wide webbing belts intended to save them from crash shock. Dane saw the pilot push the button to release fend cushions. In spite of his pounding heart, a small fraction of his brain recognized the other's skill as the Khatkan took a course to bring them down on a relatively level patch of sand and gravel.

Dane raised his head from the shelter of his folded arms. The Chief Ranger was busy with the pilot, who lay limply against the controls. Captain Jellico and Tau were already pulling at the buckles of their protective crash belts. But one look at the front of the flitter told Dane that it would not take to the air again without extensive repairs. Its nose was bent up and back, obscuring the forward view completely. However, the pilot had made a miraculously safe landing considering the terrain.

Ten minutes later, the pilot restored to consciousness and the gash in his head bandaged, they held a council of war.

"The com was off, too. I did not have a chance to report before the crash," Asaki put the situation straightly. "And our exploring parties have not yet mapped this side of the range; it has a bad reputation because of the swamp."

Jellico measured the heights now to their west with resigned eyes. "Looks as if we climb."

"Not here," the Chief Ranger corrected him. "There is no passing through the crater lake region on foot. We must travel south along the edge of the mountain area until we do find a scalable way into the preserve region."

"You seem very certain we are not going to be rescued if we stay right here," Tau observed. "Why?"

"Because I'm inclined to believe that any flitter that tries to reach us may run into the same trouble. Also, they have no com fix on us. It will be at least a day or more before they will even begin to count us missing, and then they will have the whole northern portion of the preserve to comb; there are not enough men here—I can give you a multitude of reasons, Medic."

"One of which might be sabotage?" demanded Jellico.

Asaki shrugged. "Perhaps. I am not loved in some quarters. But there may also be something fatal to flitters here as there is over Mygra. We thought the crater lake district safely beyond the swamp influence, but it may not be so."

But you took the chance of traveling over it, Dane thought, though he did not comment aloud. Was this another of the Chief Ranger's attempts to involve them in some private trouble of his own? Though to deliberately smash up a flitter and set them all afoot in this wilderness was a pretty drastic move.

Asaki had started to unload emergency supplies from the flitter. They each had a trail bag for a pack. But when the pilot staggered over to pull out a set of stass belts and Jellico began to uncoil them, the Chief Ranger shook his head.

"With the feeder beam shut off by the mountains, I fear those will no longer work."

Jellico tossed one on the crumpled nose of the flitter and punched its button with the tip of the needler barrel. Then he threw a rock at the dangling belt. The stone landed, taking the wide protective band with it to the ground. That force field which should have warded off the missile was not working.

"Oh, fine!" Tau opened his trail bag to pack concentrates. Then he smiled crookedly. "We aren't signed in for killing licenses, sir. Do you pay our fines if we are forced to shoot a hole through something that disputes the right of way?"

To Dane's surprise, the Chief Ranger laughed. "You are off preserve now, Medic Tau. The rules do not cover wild land. But I would suggest we now hunt a cave before nightfall."

"Lions?" asked Jellico.

Dane, remembering the black and white beast Lumbrilo had presented, did not enjoy that thought. They had—his gaze went from man to man checking weapons—the needler Asaki carried, and another the pilot had slung by its carrying strap over his shoulder. Tau and the captain both were armed with blasters and he had a fire ray and a force blade, both considered small arms but deadly enough perhaps even to dampen a lion's enthusiasm for the chase.

"Lions, graz, rock apes," Asaki fastened the mouth of his trail bag. "All are hunters or killers. The graz send out scouts, and they are big and formidable enough to have no enemies. Lions hunt with intelligence and skill. Rock apes are dangerous, but luckily they cannot keep silent when they scent their prey and so give one warning."

As they climbed up-slope from the flitter, Dane, looking back, saw that perhaps Asaki was right in his belief that they had better try to help themselves rather than wait for rescue. Putting aside the excuse of fearing another crack-up, the wrecked flitter made no outstanding mark on the ground. The higher they climbed, the less it could be distinguished from the tumble of rocks about it.

He had lagged a little behind and, when he hurried to catch up, found Jellico standing with his distance vision lenses to his eyes, directing them toward that shadow marking the swamp. As the younger spaceman reached him, the captain lowered the glasses and spoke:

"Take your knife, Thorson, and hold it close to that rock—over there." He pointed to a rounded black knob protruding from the soil a little off their path.

Dane obeyed, only to have the blade jerk in his hand. And when he loosened his hold in amazement, the steel slapped tight against the stone.

"Magnetic!"

"Yes. Which might explain our crash. Also this." Jellico held out a field compass to demonstrate that its needle had gone completely mad.

"We can use the mountain range itself for a guide," Dane said with more confidence than he felt.

"True enough. But we may have trouble when we head west again." Jellico let the lenses swing free on their cord about his neck. "If we were wrecked on purpose"—his mouth tightened and the old blaster burn on his cheek stretched as did his jaw set—"then someone is going to answer a lot of questions—and fast!"

"The Chief Ranger, sir?"

"I don't know. I just don't know!" The captain grunted as he adjusted his pack and started on.

If fortune had failed them earlier, she smiled on them now. Asaki discovered a cave before sundown, located not too far from a mountain stream. The Ranger sniffed the air before that dark opening as the Hunter pilot shed his equipment and crept forward on his hands and knees, his head up and his nostrils expanding as he, too, tested the scent from the cave mouth.

Scent? It was closer to a stench, and one ripe enough to turn the stomach of an off-worlder. But the Hunter glanced back over his shoulder and nodded reassuringly.

"Lion. But old. Not here within five days at least."

"Well enough. And even old lion scent will keep away rock apes. We'll clean some and then we can rest undisturbed," was his superior's comment.

The cleaning was easy for the brittle bedding of dried bracken and grass the beast had left burned quickly, cleansing with both fire and smoke. When they raked the ashes out with branches, Asaki and Nymani brought in handfuls of leaves which they crumpled and threw on the floor, spreading an aromatic odor which banished most of the foulness.

Dane, at the stream with the canteens to fill, chanced upon a small pool where there was a spread of smooth yellow sand. Knowing well the many weird booby traps one might stumble into on a strange world, the Terran prospected carefully, stirring up the stand with a stick. Sighting not so much as a water insect or a curious fish, he pulled off his boots, rolled up his breeches and waded in. The water was cool and refreshing, though he dared not drink it until the purifier was added. Then, with the filled canteens knotted together by their straps, he put on his boots and climbed to the cave where Tau waited with water tablets.

Half an hour later Dane sat cross-legged by the fire, turning a spit strung with three small birds Asaki had brought in. One foot closer to the heat began to tingle and he eased off his boot; his cramped toes suddenly seeming to have doubled in size. He was staring wide-eyed at these same toes, puffed, red, and increasingly painful to the touch, when Nymani squatted beside him, inspected his foot closely, and ordered him to take off his other boot.

"What is it?" Dane found that shedding the other boot was a minor torture in itself.

Nymani was cutting tiny splinters, hardly thicker than a needle, from a stick.

"Sand worm—lays eggs in flesh. We burn them out or you have bad foot."

"Burn them out!" Dane echoed, and then swallowed as he watched Nymani advance a splinter to the fire.

"Burn them," the Khatkan repeated firmly. "Burn tonight, hurt some tomorrow; all well soon. No burn—very bad."

Dane ruefully prepared to pay the consequences of his first brush with the unpleasant surprises Khatka had to offer.

IV

Dane regarded his throbbing feet morosely. Nymani's operations with burning splinters had been hard to take, but he had endured them without disgracing himself before the Khatkans, who appeared to regard such a mishap as just another travel incident. Now, with Tau's salve soothing the worst of the after affects, the Terran was given time to reflect upon his own stupidity and the fact that he might now prove a drag on the whole party the next morning.

"That's queer...."

Dane was startled out of the contemplation of his misery to see the medic on his knees before their row of canteens, the vial of water purifier held to the firelight for a closer inspection.

"What's the matter?"

"We must have hit with a pretty hard thump back there. Some of these pills are powder! Have to guess about the portion to add." With the tip of his knife blade Tau scraped a tiny amount of pill fragments into each waiting canteen. "That should do it. But if the water tastes a little bitter, don't let it bother you."

Bitter water, Dane thought, trying to flex his still swollen toes, was going to be the least of his worries in the morning. But he determined that his boots should go on at daybreak, and he would keep on his feet as long as the others did, no matter how much it cost him.

And when they set out shortly after daybreak, wanting to move as far as they could before the heat hours when they must rest, the going was not too bad. Dane's feet were tender to the touch, but he could shuffle along at the tail of the procession with only Nymani playing rear guard behind him.

Jungle lay before them and bush knives began to swing, clearing their path. Dane took his turn with the rest at that chore, thankful that the business of cutting their way through that mass of greenery slowed them to a pace he could match—if not in comfort, then by willpower.

But the sand worms were not the only troubles one could encounter on Khatka. Within an hour Captain Jellico stood sweating and speaking his mind freely in the native tongues of five different planets while Tau and Nymani worked as a team with skinning knives. They were not flaying the spaceman, but they came near to that in places as they worried a choice selection of tree thorns out of his arm and shoulder. The captain had been unfortunate enough to trip and fall into the embrace of a very unfriendly bush.

Dane inspected a fallen tree for evidence of inimical wild life, and then rested his blanket between him and it as a protecting cushion before he sat down. These trees were not the towering giants of the true forests, but rather oversized bushes which had been made into walls by twined vines. Brilliant bursts of flowers were splotches of vivid color, and the attendant insect life was altogether too abundant. Dane tried to tally his immunity shots and hoped for the best. At the moment he wondered why anyone would want to visit Khatka, let alone pay some astronomical sum for the privilege. Though he could also guess that the plush safari arranged for a paying client might be run on quite different lines from their own present trek.

How could a tracker find his way through this? With the compasses playing crazy tricks into the bargain! Jellico knew that the compasses were off, yet the captain had followed Asaki's lead without question, so he must trust the Ranger's forest craft. But Dane wished they were clear on the mountain side again.

Time had little meaning in that green gloom. But when they worked through to meet rock walls again, the sun said it was well into the after part of the day. They sheltered for a breather under the drooping limbs of one of the last trees.

"Amazing!" Jellico, his torn arm in a sling across his chest, came down-slope from the higher point where he had been using the distance lenses. "We struck straight across and cut off about ten miles by that jungle jog. Now I believe all that I've heard of your people's ability to cross wilderness and not lose their built in 'riding beams,' sir. With the compasses out, I'll admit I've been nourishing a healthy set of doubts."

Asaki laughed. "Captain, I do not question your ability to flit from world to world, or how you have learned to set up trade with strange humans and non-humans alike. To each his own mystery. On Khatka every boy before he becomes a man must learn to navigate the jungle, and with no instruments to help him, only what lies in here." He touched his thumb to his forehead. "So through generations we have developed our homing instincts. Those who did not, also did not live to father others who might have had the same lack. We are hounds who can run on a scent, and we are migrators who have better than a compass within our own bodies."

"Now we take to climbing again?" Tau surveyed the way before them critically.

"Not at this hour. That sun on the upward slopes can cook a man's skin were he to touch any rock. We wait...."

Waiting for the Khatkans was a chance to sleep. They curled up on their light blankets. But the three spacemen were restless. Dane would have liked to have taken off his boots, but feared he could not replace them; and he could tell from the way the captain shifted his position that Jellico was in pain too. Tau sat quietly, staring at nothing Dane could see, unless it was a tall rock thrust out of the slope like a finger pointing skyward.

"What color is that rock?"

Surprised, Dane gave the stony finger closer attention. To him it was the same color as most of the other rocks, a weathered black which in certain lights appeared to carry a brownish film.

"Black, or maybe dark brown?"

Tau looked past him to Jellico. The captain nodded.

"I'd agree with that."

Tau cupped his hands over his eyes for a moment and his lips moved as if he were counting. Then he took his hands away and stared up-slope. Dane watched the medic's eyelids blink slowly. "Nothing but black or brown?" Tau pressed.

"No." Jellico supported his injured arm upon his knees, leaning forward, as intent upon the designated rock as if he expected it to assume some far more startling appearance.

"Queer," Tau said to himself, and then added briskly, "You're right, of course. That sun can play tricks with one's eyes."

Dane continued to watch the finger rock. Maybe strong sunlight could play tricks, but he could see nothing odd about that rough lump. And since the captain asked no questions of Tau, he did not quite want to either.

It was perhaps a half-hour later, and the medic and Jellico had both succumbed to the quiet, the heat, and their own fatigue, when Dane did sight a movement up-slope. The throbbing in his feet was worse now that he had nothing to occupy his mind but his own troubles, and he was sitting facing the finger rock.

Was that what Tau had seen earlier? That quick movement around the side of the rough pillar? But if so, why the question of color? There it was again! And now, centering all his attention on that one point, the Terran picked out the outline of a head—a head grotesque enough to be something conjured out of Lumbrilo's sorcerer's imagination. Had Dane not seen its like among the tri-dee prints in Captain Jellico's collection, he would have believed that his eyes were playing tricks.

It was a bullet-shaped head, embellished by two out-sized prick ears, the hair-tufted pointed tips of which projected well above the top of the skull. Round eyes were set deeply in sunken pits. The mouth was a swinish snout from which lolled a purple tongue, though the rest of that gargoyle head was very close in color to the rock against which it half rested.

Dane had no doubts that the rock ape was spying upon the small camp. Having heard tales of those semi-intelligent animals—the most intelligent native creatures of Khatka—most of which were concerned with their more malignant characteristics, Dane was alarmed. That lurker could be an advance scout of some pack.

And a pack of rock apes, if able to surprise their prey, were formidable opponents.

Asaki stirred, sat up. And that round head above turned to follow the Chief Ranger's every move.

"Above ... by the finger rock ... to the right...." Dane kept his voice close to a whisper. When he saw the sudden constriction of muscle across the Khatkan's bare shoulders, he knew that the other had heard and understood.

Only, if Asaki had spotted the rock ape, he did not betray his knowledge. The Khatkan got lithely to his feet. Then one of those feet stirred Nymani into the instant wakefulness of the wilderness-trained man.

Dane slid his hand about the bole of the tree and touched Jellico, watched the captain's gray eyes open with a similar awareness. Asaki picked up his needler. Weapon in hand, he whirled and fired almost in one connected movement. It was the fastest shot Dane had ever seen.

The gargoyle head lifted away from the rock, and then turned to one side as its body, somehow vaguely obscene in its resemblance to the human form, fell away, to sprawl limply down-slope.

Though the dead rock ape had not had a chance to give tongue, there came a cry from above, a coughing, deep-throated hawking. Down the steep incline bumped a round white ball, bouncing past the tumbled carcass of the ape, sailing up into the air, to strike and burst open a few feet away.

"Back!" With one arm Asaki sent Jellico, his nearest neighbor, tumbling back into the jungle. Then the Chief Ranger pumped a stream of needle rays into the remains of the ball. A shrill, sweet humming arose as red motes, vivid as molten copper in the sunlight, climbed on wings beating too fast to be seen.

The debris of the nest smoked into nothing. But no needle ray could hope to stop all the poisonous army issuing forth from it, fighting mad, to seek any warm-blooded creature within scenting distance. The men threw themselves into the brush, rolling in the thick mold of the vegetable decay on the ground, rubbing its moist plaster over their bodies in frantic haste.

Red-hot fire, far worse than any of the splinter torment Dane had undergone the night before, pierced between his shoulders. He rolled on his back, shoving himself along, both to kill the fire-wasp and coat the sting with cooling mold. Cries of pain told him that he was not the only sufferer, as all dug hands into the slimy stuff under them and slapped it over their faces and heads.

"Apes...." That half shout got through to alert the men on the jungle floor. True to their nature, the rock apes, now streaming downhill, were coughing their challenges, advertising their attack. And it was only that peculiarity of their species which saved their intended victims.

The apes came forward, partially erect, at a shambling run. The first two, bulls close to six feet, went down under fire from Asaki's needler. A third somehow escaped, swerving to the left, and came bounding at an angle toward Dane. The Terran jerked free his force blade as that swine snout split wide to show greenish tusks and the horrible stench of the creature's body made him gasp.

A taloned paw clawed at him eagerly, slipped from his slime-covered body just as he brought the force blade up. Foul breath coughed in his face and he stumbled back as the heavy body of the ape crashed against him, cut in half by the weapon. To Dane's sickened horror the paws still clawed for him, the fangs still gnashed as he rolled free of the mangled body and somehow got to his feet.

The roar of a blaster, of two blasters, drowned out the clamor of the apes as Dane drew his fire ray, set his shoulders against a tree bole and prepared to fight it out. He fired, saw a smaller and more nimble enemy go down screeching. Then there were none left on their shaggy feet, though some on the ground dragged themselves forward, still striving to reach the men.

Dane slapped a fire-wasp from his leg. He was glad of the support of the tree at his back as the smell of the ape's blood drenching him from chest level down, and the mess on the ground, made his stomach churn.

When he could control his retching, he straightened. To his relief he saw that all the others were on their feet, apparently unharmed. But Tau, catching sight of the younger spaceman, gasped and started for him.

"Dane! What did they do?"

His junior laughed a little hysterically. "Not mine...." He swabbed with a handful of grass at his bloodied breeches and blundered on into the sunlight.

Nymani found them a foam-flecked stream below a miniature falls where the swift current prevented the lurking of sand worms. They stripped eagerly, cleaning first themselves and then their fouled clothing while Tau tended the wealth of fire-wasp stings.

There was little he could do to relieve the swelling and pain, until Asaki produced a reed-like plant which, chopped in sections, yielded a sticky purple liquid that dried on the skin as a tar gum—the native remedy. So, glued and plastered, they climbed away from the water and prepared to spend the night in a hollow between two leaning rocks, certainly not as snug as the cave but a fortress of sorts.

"And credit-happy space hoppers pay a fortune for an outing like this!" Tau commented bitterly, hunching well forward so that a certain stung portion of his anatomy would not come in contact with the rock beneath him.

"Hardly for this," Jellico replied, and Dane saw Nymani grin one-sidedly, his other cheek puffed and painted sticky purple.

"We do not always encounter apes and fire-wasps in the same day," supplied the Chief Ranger. "Also, guests at the preserves wear stass belts."

Jellico snorted. "I don't think you'd get any repeats from your clients otherwise! What do we meet tomorrow? A herd of graz on stampede, or something even more subtle and deadly?"

Nymani got up and walked a little way from their rock shelter. He turned down-slope and Dane saw his nostrils expand as they had when he had investigated the cave.

"Something is dead," he said slowly. "A very large something. Or else—"

Asaki strode down to join his men. He gave a curt nod and Nymani skidded on down the mountain side.

"What is it?" Jellico asked.

"It might be many things. There is one I hope it is not," was the Chief Ranger's somewhat evasive reply. "I will hunt a labbla—there was fresh spoor at the stream." He set off along their back trail to return a half hour later, the body of his kill slung across one shoulder. He was skinning it when Nymani trotted back.

"Well?"

"Death pit," supplied the Hunter.

"Poachers?" Jellico inquired.

Nymani nodded. Asaki continued his task, but there was a glint in his dark eyes as he butchered with sure and expert strokes. Then he glanced at the shadow extending beyond the rocks.

"I, too, would see," he told Nymani.

Jellico arose, and Dane, interested, followed. Some five minutes later none of them needed the native keenness of smell to detect the presence of some foulness ahead. The odor of corruption was almost tangible in the sultry air. And it grew worse until they stood on the edge of a pit. Dane retreated hurriedly. This was as bad as the battlefield of the rock apes. But the captain and the two Khatkans stood calmly assessing the slaughter left by the hide poachers.

"Glam, graz, hoodra," Jellico commented. "Tusks and hides—the full line of trade stuff."

Asaki, his expression bleak, stepped back from the pit. "Day old calves, old ones, females—all together. They kill wantonly and leave those they do not choose to pelt."

"Trail—" Nymani pointed eastward. "Leads to Mygra swamp."

"The swamps!" Asaki was shaken. "They must be mad!"

"Or know more about this country than your men do," Jellico corrected.

"If poachers can enter Mygra, then we can follow!"

But not now, Dane protested silently. Certainly Asaki did not mean that they were to track outlaws into swamps the Khatkan had already labeled unexplored death traps!

V

Sitting up, Dane stared wide-eyed into the dark. A handful of glowing coals, guarded by rocks, was the center of their camp. He hunched up to that hardly knowing why he moved. His hands were shaking, his skin damp with sweat no heat produced. Yet, now that he was conscious of the night, the Terran could not remember the nightmare from which he had just awakened, though he was left with a growing apprehension which he could not define. What prowled out there in that dark? Walked the mountain side? Listened, spied and waited?

Dane half started to his feet as a form did move into the dim light of the fire. Tau stood there, regarding him with sober intensity.

"Bad dream?"

The younger man admitted to that with a nod, partly against his will.

"Well, you aren't the only one. Remember any of it?"

With an effort, Dane looked away from the encircling dark. It was as if the fear which had shaken him awake, now embodied, lurked right there.

"No." He rubbed sleep-smarting eyes.

"Neither did I," Tau remarked. "But both of 'em must have been jet-powered."

"I suppose one could expect to have nightmares after yesterday." Dane advanced the logical explanation, yet at the same time

55

something deep inside him denied every word of it. He had known nightmares before; none of them had left this aftertaste. And he wanted no return of sleep tonight. Reaching to the pile of wood he fed the fire as Tau settled down beside him.

"There is something else...." the medic began, and then fell silent. Dane did not press him. The younger man was too busy fighting a growing desire to whirl and aim the fire ray into that darkness, to catch in its withering blast that lurking thing he could feel padded there, biding its time.

Despite his efforts Dane did drowse again before morning, waking unrefreshed, and, to his secret dismay, with no lessening of his odd dislike for the country about them.

Asaki did not suggest that they trail the poachers into the morass of Mygra. Instead the Chief Ranger was eager to press on in the opposite direction, find a way over the range to the preserve where he could assemble a punitive force to deal with the outlaws. So they began an upward climb which took them away from the dank heat of the lowlands, into the parched blaze of the sunbaked ledges above.

The sun was bright, far too bright, and there were few shadows left. Yet Dane, stopping to drink sparingly from his canteen, could not lose that sense of eyes upon him, of being tracked. Rock apes? Cunning as those beasts were, it was against their nature to trail in utter silence, to be able to carry through a long-term project. Lion, perhaps?

He noted that Nymani and Asaki took turns at rear guard today, and that each was alert. Yet, oddly enough, none of them mentioned the uneasiness they must all share.

They had a dry climb, finding no mountain stream to renew their water supply. All being experienced in wilderness travel, they made a mouthful of liquid go a long way. When the party halted slightly before midday, canteens were still half full.

"Haugh!"

They jerked up, hands on weapons. A rock ape, its hideous body clearly seen here, capered, coughed, spat. Asaki fired from the hip and the thing screeched, clawed at its chest where the dark blood spewed out, and raced for them. Nymani cut the beast down and they waited tensely for the attack of the thing's tribe, which should have followed the abortive lunge on the part of their scout. But there was nothing—neither sound nor movement.

What did follow froze them all momentarily. That mangled body began to move again, drew itself together, crawled toward them. Dane knew that it was impossible that the creature could live with such wounds. Yet the beast advanced, its head lolling on its hunched shoulders so that the eyes were turned blindly up to the full glare of the sun, while it crawled to reach the man it could not see.

"Demon!" Nymani dropped his needler, shrank back against the rocks.

As the thing advanced, before their eyes the impossible happened. Those gaping wounds closed, the head straightened on the almost invisible neck, the eyes glared once more with life, and slaver dripped from the swine snout.

Jellico caught up the needler Nymani had dropped. With a coolness Dane envied, the captain shot. And for the second time the rock ape collapsed, torn to ribbons.

Nymani screamed, and Dane tried to choke back his own cry of horrified protest. The dead thing put on life for the second time, crawled, got somehow to its feet, healed itself, and came on. Asaki, his face greenish-pale, stepped out stiffly as if each step he took was forced by torture. He had dropped his needler. Now he caught up a rock as large as his own head, raised it high with arms on which the muscles stood out like ropes. He hurled the stone, and Dane heard as well as saw the missile go home. The rock ape fell for the third time.

When one of those taloned paws began to move again, Nymani broke. He ran, his screams echoing thinly in the air, as the thing lurched up, the gory mess of its head weaving about. If his feet would have obeyed him, Dane might have followed the Khatkan. As it was, he drew his ray and aimed it at that shambling thing. Tau struck up the barrel.

The medic's face was livid; there was the same horror in his eyes. But he moved out to front that monster.

A spot of shadow coalesced on the ground, deepened in hue, took on substance. Crouched low facing the rock ape, its haunches quivering for a deadly spring, narrowed green eyes holding on its prey, was a black leopard.

The tiny forward and backward movements of its body steadied, and it arched through the air, brought down the ape. A pitting, snarling tangle rolled across the slope—and was gone!

Asaki's hands shook as he drew them down his sweating face. Jellico readied a second clip in the needler mechanically. But Tau was swaying so that Dane leaped to take the shock of the other's weight as he collapsed. Only for a moment did the medic hang so, then he struggled to stand erect.

"Magic?" Jellico's voice, as controlled as ever, broke the silence.

"Mass hallucination," Tau corrected him. "Very strong."

"How!" Asaki swallowed and began again. "How was it done?"

The medic shook his head. "Not by the usual methods, that is certain. And it worked on us—on me—when we weren't conditioned. I don't understand that!"

Dane could hardly believe it yet. He watched Jellico stride to where the tangle of struggling beasts had rolled, saw him examine bare ground on which no trace of the fight remained. They must accept Tau's explanation; it was the only sane one.

Asaki's features were suddenly convulsed with a rage so stark that Dane realized how much a veneer was the painfully built civilization of Khatka.

"Lumbrilo!" The Chief Ranger made of that name a curse. Then with a visible effort he controlled his emotions and came to Tau, looming over the slighter medic almost menacingly.

"How?" he demanded for the second time.

"I don't know."

"He will try again?"

"Not the same perhaps—"

But Asaki had already grasped the situation, was looking ahead.

"We shall not know," he breathed, "what is real, what is not."

"There is also this," Tau warned. "The unreal can kill the believer just as quickly as the real!"

"That I know also. It has happened too many times lately. If we could only find out how! Here are no drums, no singing—none of the tricks to tangle a man's mind that he usually uses to summon his demons. So without Lumbrilo, without his witch tools, how does he make us see what is not?"

"That we must discover and speedily, sir. Or else we shall be lost among the unreal and the real."

"You also have the power. You can save us!" Asaki protested.

Tau drew his arm across his face. Very little of the normal color had returned to his thin, mobile features. He still leaned against Dane's supporting arm.

"A man can do only so much, sir. To battle Lumbrilo on his own ground is exhausting and I can not fight so very often."

"But will he not also be exhausted?"

"I wonder...." Tau gazed beyond the Khatkan to the barren ground where leopard and rock ape had ceased to be. "This magic is a tricky thing, sir. It builds and feeds upon a man's own imagination and inner fears. Lumbrilo, having triggered ours, need not strive at all, but let us ourselves raise that which will attack us."

"Drugs?" demanded Jellico.

Tau gave a start sufficient to take him out of Dane's loose hold.

His hand went to the packet of aid supplies which was his own care, his eyes round with wonder and then shrewdly alert.

"Captain, we disinfected those thorn punctures of yours. Thorson, your foot salve.... But, no, I didn't use anything—"

"You forget, Craig, we all had scratches after that fight with the apes."

Tau sat down on the ground. With feverish haste he unsealed his medical supplies, laid out some containers. Then delicately he opened each, examined its contents closely by eye, by smell, and two by taste. When he was done he shook his head.

"If these have been in any way meddled with, I would need laboratory analysis to detect it. And I don't believe that Lumbrilo could hide traces of his work so cleverly. Or has he been off-planet? Had much to do with off-worlders?" he asked the Chief Ranger.

"By the nature of his position he is forbidden to space voyage, to have any close relationship with any off-worlder. I do not think, medic, he would choose your healing substances for his mischief. There would only be chance to aid him then in producing the effects he wants. Though there is often call for first aid in travel, he could not be certain you would use any of your drugs on this trip to the preserve."

"And Lumbrilo was certain. He threatened something such as this," Jellico reminded them.

"So it would be something which we would all use, which we had to depend upon...."

"The water!" Dane had been holding his own canteen ready to drink. But as that possible explanation dawned in his mind, he smelled instead of tasted the liquid sloshing inside. There was no odor he could detect. But he remembered Tau commenting on the powdered purifier pills at their first camp.

"That's it!" Tau dug further into his kit, brought out the vial of white powder with its grainy lumps. Pouring a little into the palm of his hand he smelled it, touched it with the tip of his tongue. "Purifier and something else," he reported. "It could be one of half a dozen drugs, or some native stuff from here which we've never classified."

"True. There are drugs we have found here." Asaki scowled down at the green mat of jungle. "So our water is poisoned?"

"Do you always purify it?" Tau asked the Chief Ranger. "Surely during the centuries since your ancestors landed on Khatka you must have adapted to native water. You couldn't have lived otherwise. We must use the purifier, but must you?"

"There is water and water." Asaki shook his own canteen, his scowl growing fiercer as the gurgle from its depths was heard. "From springs on the other side of the mountains we drink—yes. But over here, this close to the Mygra swamps, we have not done so. We may have to chance it."

"Do you think we are literally poisoned?" Jellico bored directly to the heart of their private fears.

"None of us have been drinking too heavily," Tau observed thoughtfully. "And I don't believe Lumbrilo had outright killing in mind. How long the effect will last I have no way of telling."

"If we saw one rock ape," Dane wondered, "why didn't we see others? And why here and now?"

"That!" Tau pointed ahead on the trail Asaki had picked for their ascent. For a long moment Dane could see nothing of any interest there and then he located it—a finger of rock. It did not point directly skyward this time, in fact it slanted so that its tip indicated their back trail. Yet in outline the spire was very similar to that outcrop from which the real rock ape had charged them the day before.

Asaki exclaimed in his own tongue and slapped his hand hard against the stock of the needler.

"We saw that and so again we saw an ape also! Had earlier we been charged by graz or jumped by a lion in such a place, then again we would have been faced by graz or lion here!"

Captain Jellico gave a bark of laughter colored only by the most sardonic humor. "Clever enough. He merely leaves it to us to select our own ghost and then repeat the performance in the next proper setting. I wonder how many rocks shaped like that one there are in these mountains? And how long will a rock ape continue to pop out from behind each one we do find?"

"Who knows? But as long as we drink this water we're going to continue to have trouble; I feel safe in promising that," Tau replied. He put the vial of doctored purifier into a separate pocket of his medical kit. "It may be a problem of how long we can go without water."

"Perhaps," Asaki said softly. "Only not all the water on Khatka comes running in streams."

"Fruit?" Tau asked.

"No, trees. Lumbrilo is not a hunter, nor could he be certain when and where his magic would go to work. Unless the flitter was deliberately sabotaged, he was planning for us to use our canteens in the preserve. That is lion country and there are long distances between springs. This is jungle below us and there is a source there I think we can safely tap. But first I must find Nymani and prove to him that this is truly deviltry of a sort, but not demon inspired."

He was gone, running lightly down-slope in the direction his hunter had taken, and Dane spoke to Captain Jellico.

"What's this about water in trees, sir?"

"There is a species of tree here, not too common, with a thickened trunk. It stores water during the rainy season to live on in the hot months. Since we are in the transition period between rains, we could tap it—if we locate one of the trees. How about that, Tau? Dare we drink that without a purifier?"

"Probably a choice of two evils, sir. But we have had our preventive shots. Personally, I'd rather battle disease than take a chance on a mind-twisting drug. You can go without water just so long...."

"I'd like to have a little talk with Lumbrilo," remarked Jellico, the mildness in his voice very deceptive.

"I'm going to have a little talk with Lumbrilo, if and when we see him again!" promised Tau.

"What are our chances, sir?" Dane asked. He screwed the cap back on his canteen, his mouth feeling twice as dry since he knew he dared not drink.

"Well, we've faced gambles before." Tau sealed the medical kit. "I'd like to see one of those trees before sundown. And I don't want to face another pointed rock today!"

"Why the leopard?" asked Jellico reflectively. "Another case of using flame to fight fire? But Lumbrilo wasn't among those present to be impressed."

Tau rubbed his hand across his forehead. "I don't really know, sir. Maybe I could have made the ape vanish without a counter projection, but I don't think so. With these hallucinations it is better to battle one vision against another for the benefit of those involved. And I can't even tell you why I selected a leopard—it just flashed into mind as about the fastest and most deadly animal fighter I could recall at that moment."

"You'd better work out a good list of such fighters." Jellico's grim humor showed again. "I can supply a few if you need them. Not that I don't share your hope we won't see any more trigger rocks. Here comes Asaki with his wandering boy."

The Chief Ranger was half-leading, half-supporting his hunter, and Nymani seemed only half-conscious. Tau got to his feet and hurried to meet them. It would appear that their search for the water tree would be delayed.

VI

They withdrew to a spot hacked from the edge of the jungle, leaving a screen of green between them and the traitorous up-slope. But within the few hours of daylight left them, it was proven that Asaki had been overly optimistic in his hopes of discovering a water tree. They were now in a narrow tongue of land between the range and the swamps, and this territory was limited. Nymani, still shaken, was of little help, and the spacemen did not dare to strike out into unexplored land alone.

So they mouthed dry concentrates and dared not drink. Dane was tempted to pour out the liquid in his canteen. Water so close to hand was a continual torment. And, now that they were away from the heights and the possibility of more finger-shaped rocks, surely the threat in that moisture was small in comparison to the needs of his body. Only that caution which was drilled into every Free Trader supplied a brake to his thirst.

Jellico drew the back of his hand across cracked lips. "Suppose we should draw lots—some of us drink, one or two not. Could we manage that way until we were over the mountains?"

"I wouldn't want to chance it, unless we are left with no other choice. There is no way of telling how long the drug works. Frankly, right now I'm not even sure I could detect a hallucination for very long under these conditions," was Tau's discouraging verdict.

If any of them slept that night, they did so only in snatches. The apprehension which had come with the previous night was back, intensified, and that lurking, indefinable fear rode them hard.

They were shaken out of their private terrors shortly after dawn. There were always sounds to be heard in the jungle: the cries of unseen birds, the crash of some tree eaten alive by parasitic sapping. But what broke now was no bird call, no isolated tree falling. A trumpeting roar, the crackling smash of vegetation, heralded a real menace. Asaki spun to face northward, though there was nothing to be seen there except the unshaken wall of the jungle.

"Graz! Graz on stampede!" Nymani joined his superior.

Jellico arose swiftly and Dane read on the captain's face the seriousness of this. The off-worlder turned to his own men with a sharp order. "On your feet! We may have to move on the double. Up-mountain?" he demanded of the Chief Ranger.

The other was still listening, not only with his ears but with the whole of his tense body. Three of the deer-like creatures they had hunted for food broke out of the green wall, fled past the men as if the latter was invisible. And behind them, the hunted now and not the hunter, came a lion, its strikingly marked black-and-white hide dramatic in the light of the morning. It showed fangs in a snarl and then was gone in one huge bound. More deer things, scurrying of other small creatures, moving too fast for clear identification, and behind them the fury of destruction which marked the headlong advance of Khatka's largest mammals slamming through the jungle.

They had started up-slope when Nymani cried out. A white bulk, hard to distinguish in that light against the gray of the earth, headed after them. Dane had a fleeting glimpse of curled tusks, of an open mouth, raw-red and wide enough to engulf his whole head, of shaggy legs driving at an unbelievable pace. Asaki snapped a beam from the needler. The white monster roared and came on. They dived for the scant cover offered as the graz bull died, not two yards away from the Chief Ranger, its heavy body skidding along the earth with the force of its speed as it went down.

"That did it!" Jellico sighted coolly with his blaster as a second bull, fighting mad, tore from the jungle and pounded at them. Behind it a third tusked head thrust out of the brush, large eyes searched for an enemy. Dane studied the dead bull, but the animal did not come to life this time. These were not hallucinations. And the malignancy of the rock apes, the cunning of the native Khatkan lion, were pallid things compared to a graz herd on the rampage.

The second bull yelped with an almost canine complaint as Jellico's blaster caught it head-on. Blinded, the beast blundered ahead, climbing the mountain side. The third met a ray from Nymani's needler. But the Chief Ranger leaped from behind his sheltering rock to the one where the captain had taken refuge and pulled him into the open.

"They must not corner us here!"

Jellico agreed to that. "Come on!" he barked to Tau and Dane.

They fled along a rough way, trying to gain altitude, but finding a rising cliff wall which could not be easily climbed. Two more graz went down, one badly wounded, one safely dead. Behind them more white heads came from the brush. What original cause had started the stampede the fugitives could not guess, but now the fear and anger of the animals were centering upon them.

And, in spite of their efforts, the party was being herded into a pocket between the jungle below, where the main body of graz crashed along, and a steep wall. Given time to find the necessary finger and toe holds, a man might climb that wall, but they could not attempt it now. The portion of ledge on which they ran, stopped to fire, and then ran on again, angled to the southeast. And so they came to its end quickly, a drop ending in a plain of yellow-gray mud studded with clumps of bleached vegetation which led, like steppingstones, toward a tangle of matted, sickly looking plants and reeds.

"All right," Tau faced around, "what do we do now? Space lift? And using what for wings or jets?"

As if the graz could sense that they now had their victims safely cornered, what must have been a goodly segment of the herd hooked their way from the jungle and started up. Puffing, digging in those sturdy legs which had to take the massive weight of their barrel-shaped bodies, they made their way determinedly up-grade. One might almost believe that they had intelligently planned this end for their drive.

"We go down!" Asaki yelled, and used his needler on the leader of that climbing platoon.

"The brush islands," Nymani amended. "I show you!" He thrust his needler at Jellico and was over the edge of the ledge, hanging by his hands and swinging his weight back and forth like a pendulum. At the up-swing of his body to the right, he let go and plunged out, landing half across one of the reed islets. The Khatkan clawed his way to his knees, gained his feet, and leaped for the next bit of solid ground.

"You, Thorson!" Jellico jerked his head at Dane and the younger spaceman holstered his fire ray, slipped gingerly over the drop and prepared to repeat Nymani's feat as best he could.

He was not quite as successful with his sidewise swing, landing with only his forearms across the islet, the rest of his body being swiftly embedded in what was ooze covered only with a thin crust of dried matter. The stench of the stuff was sickening, but the fear of being entrapped in it gave him the necessary impetus to push forward, though what was meant to be a swift half-dive was more of a worm's progress. He grabbed frantically at brittle stems, at coarse grass which cut like knives at his hands. But some of the material held and he lay face down on a lump which did not give under his weight.

There was no time to linger; he had to get to the next patch, to free this dubious landing place for the men embattled on the rise above. Stumbling up, Dane judged the distance with a space-trained eye and jumped to a knob Nymani had already quitted. The Khatkan was more than halfway along toward that promise of solid ground which the tangled mass of leprous vegetation led to, zigzagging expertly from islet to islet.

There was a crash and a roar behind. Dane balanced on the third of the minute islands to look back. He saw the lash of blaster fire on the top of the cliff, Tau on his knees on the first of their chain of steppingstones, and a graz sprawled head and forequarters in the sucking muck where it had dived past the two defenders above. Needler and blaster fired together again, and then Jellico swung over the cliff rim. Tau waved vigorously and Dane took off for the next islet, just making it by lucky chance.

The rest of the journey he took in a rush, trying not to think of anything but the necessity of landing on some spot of firm ground. His last leap of all was too short, so that he went knee deep in a particularly evil-smelling pool where yellow scum spattered his breeches and he experienced the insidious pull of the bottomless stuff. A stout branch whipped across his shoulder and he caught it. With Nymani's wiry strength on the other end, Dane worked free and sat, white-faced and shivering, on a mat of brush, while the Khatkan hunter turned his attention to the safety of Tau, the next arrival.

More fortunate, or more skillful than Dane, the medic made the hop from the last tuft without mishap. But he was blowing heavily as he collapsed beside the other spaceman. Together they watched the progress of their captain.

Safe on the second tussock from the shore, Jellico halted, edged carefully around and used the needler Nymani had left with him. A shaggy head tossed and the bull fronting Asaki on the cliff went down. The Chief Ranger dodged quickly to the right and a second beast rushed out and over, to join its mired comrade in the swamp below. As Jellico shot again, the Khatkan slung his needler and went over to gain the first islet.

One more graz was wounded but luckily it hunched about, turning its formidable tusks on those that followed, thus keeping the path clear for its enemies. Jellico was making the journey, sure-footedly, with the Chief Ranger only one hillock behind. Tau sighed.

"Someday maybe this will be just another tall tale and we'll all be thought liars when we spout it," he observed. "That is if we survive to tell it. So now which way do we go? If I had my choice it would be up!"

71

When Dane pulled himself to his feet and surveyed their small refuge, he was ready to agree to that. For the space, packed with dead and dying vegetable matter until one sank calf deep, was a triangle with a narrow point running east into the swamp.

"They don't give up easily, do they?" Jellico looked back to the shore and the cliff. Though the wounded graz bull still held the heights against its fellows, there were others breaking from the jungle on the lower level, wandering back and forth to paw the earth, rip up soil with their tusks, and otherwise threaten anyone who would try to return to the strip they patrolled.

"They will not," Asaki answered bleakly. "Arouse a graz and it will trail you for days; kill any of the herd and you have little hope of escaping them on foot."

It would seem now that the swamp was a deterrent to pursuit. The two beasts that had fallen in the mire moaned in a pitiful rising note. They had ceased to struggle and several of their kind clustered on the shore near them, calling entreatingly. Asaki took careful aim with the needler and put one animal after another out of its misery. But the flash of those shots angered those on shore to a higher pitch of rage.

"No going back," he said. "At least not for several days."

Tau slapped a black, four-winged insect which had settled on his arm, its jaws wide open for a sampling bite. "We can't very well perch here until they forget all about us," he pointed out. "Not without water we can trust, and with the local wild life ready to test us for tasty eating."

Nymani had prowled along the swampward point of their island, and now he made his report.

72

"There is more high land to the east. Perhaps it will give us a bridge across."

At that moment Dane doubted his ability to make any more leaps from island to island. And it would seem Tau shared his discouragement.

"I don't suppose you could discourage our friends on shore there with a few more shots?"

Asaki shook his head. "We do not have clips enough to settle a whole herd. These might retreat from sight but they would be waiting for us in the bush, and that would mean certain death. We shall have to take the swamp road."

If Dane had considered their earlier march misery, this was sheer torture. Since footing was never secure, falls were frequent, and within a quarter-hour they were all plastered with evil-smelling slime and mud which hardened to rock consistency when exposed to the air. Painful as this was, it did protect a portion of their bodies from the insects with which the swamp was well stocked.

And, in spite of their efforts to find a way out, the only possible paths led them deeper into the center of the unexplored morass. At last Asaki called a halt and a council to consider retreat. To locate an island from which they could at least watch the shore appealed very strongly indeed.

"We have to have water." Tau's voice was a harsh croak, issuing out of a mask of green mud festooned with trailing weeds.

"This ground is rising." Asaki smacked the stock of his needler against the surface on which he crouched. "I think perhaps there may be clean land soon to come."

Jellico hitched his way up a sapling, now bending under his weight. Through the vision lenses he studied the route ahead.

"You're right about that," he called to the Chief Ranger. "There's a showing of the right sort of green to the left, about half a mile on. And," he glanced about at the westering sun, "we have about an hour yet of good light in which to make it. I wouldn't try such a run after dark."

That promise of green bolstered their weary spirits for a last exhausting effort. Once again they were faced with a series of islet leaps, and now they carried with them brush culled from the bigger tussocks to aid in times of need.

When Dane scrambled up the last pull, staggered, and went down to his knees again, he knew he was done. He did not even move at an excited cry from Nymani, echoed a moment later by Asaki. It was not until the latter leaned over him, a canteen open in his hand, that Dane aroused a little.

"Drink!" the Khatkan urged. "We have found a water tree. This is fresh."

The liquid might have been fresh, but it also had a peculiar taste, which Dane did not note until he had gulped down a generous swallow. At that moment he was past caring about anything but the fact that he did have a portion of drinkable stuff in hand.

Here the stunted, unnatural growth of the swamplands had given away to the more normal vegetation of the jungle-clad lowlands. Had they come clear across the swamp, Dane wondered dully, or was this only a large island in the midst of the stinking boglands?

He drank again and regained strength enough to crawl to where

74

his shipmates lay. It was some time before he was interested in much besides the fact that he could drink when he wished. Then he watched Jellico waver to his feet, his head turned eastward. Tau, too, sat up as if alerted by the Queen's alarm buzzer.

The Khatkans were gone, perhaps back to the water tree. But all three of the spacemen heard that sound, a far off throbbing rhythm which was a vibration as well. Jellico looked to Tau.

"Drums?"

"Could be." The medic screwed the cap back on his canteen. "I'd say we have company—only I'd like to know what kind!"

They might have been mistaken about the drums, but none of them could have been mistaken about the bolt which came out of nowhere to slice through a tree trunk as a knife might slash wet clay. Blaster—and a particular type of blaster!

"Patrol issue!" Tau lay flat, squeezing himself against the earth as if he wished he could ooze into it.

Jellico wriggled toward the bush in answer to a low call from Asaki, and the others made a worm's progress in his wake. Under cover they found the Chief Ranger readying his needler.

"Poacher camp here," he explained bleakly. "And they know about us."

"A perfect end to a stinking day," remarked Tau dispassionately. "We might have guessed something of this sort was waiting." He tried to rub away some of the dried clay coating his chin. "But do poachers use drums?"

The Chief Ranger scowled. "That is what Nymani has gone to find out."

VII

Darkness closed in while they waited for Nymani's return. There had been no further attack from the blaster wielder; perhaps he was only trying to pin them down where they were. Out over the swamp, weird patches of phosphorescence moved in small ghostly clouds, and bright dots of insects with their own built-in lighting systems flashed spark-fashion or sailed serenely on regular flight plans. At night the wonder of the place was far removed from the squalid reality of the day. They chewed on their rations, drank sparingly of the water, and tried to keep alert to any sight or sound.

That monotonous undertone, which might or might not be drums, continued as a basic hum to the noises of the night, drowned out at intervals by a splash, a mutter or cry from some swamp creature. Beside Dane, Jellico stiffened, moved his blaster, as someone wriggled through the brush, trilling softly.

"Off-worlders," Nymani reported in gasps to Asaki, "and outlaws, too. They make a hunting sing—tomorrow they march for a killing."

Asaki rested his chin on his broad forearm. "Outlaws?"

"They show no lord's badge. But each I saw wears a bracelet of three, five, or ten tails. They are Trackers indeed, and Hunters of the best!"

"They have huts?"

"Not so. There are no dwellers in the inners courts here." Out of habit Nymani used the polite term for the women of his race. "I would say they tarry only for the space of a hunt. And on the boots of one I saw salt crust."

"Salt crust!" Asaki snapped and half arose. "So that is the type of lure they use. There must be a saline mire near here to pull game—"

"How many off-worlders?" Jellico broke in.

"Three who are Hunters, one who is different."

"How different?" questioned Asaki.

"He wears upon his body garments which are strange; on his head a round covering such as we see upon the off-worlders of the ships—"

"A spaceman!"

Asaki laughed harshly. "Why not? They must have some method of transporting their hides."

"You can't tell me," Jellico returned, "that anyone is able to set a ship down in this muck. It would simply be buried for all time."

"But, Captain, what type of a spaceport does a Free Trader need? Do you not planet your own ship on worlds where there are no waiting cradles, no fitter shops, none of the conveniences such as mark the field Combine maintains on Xecho?"

"Of course I do. But one does need a reasonably smooth stretch of territory, open enough so the tail flames won't start a forest fire. You don't ever ride a tail push down in a swamp!"

"Which testifies to a trail out of here, fairly well-traveled, and some kind of a usable landing space not too far away," Asaki replied. "And that could very well serve us."

"But they know we are here," Tau pointed out.

It was Nymani's turn to laugh. "Man from the stars, there is no trail so well-hidden that a Ranger of the preserves cannot nose it out, nor any Hunter—be he a two or five bracelet veteran—who can keep pinned down a determined man of the forest service!"

Dane lost interest in the argument at that moment. He was at the edge of their line, the nearest to the swamp, and he had been watching patches of ghostly light flitting above the rank water-weeds. For the past few moments those wisps of faded radiance had been gathering into a growing anthropomorphic blot hanging over the morass several yards away. And the misty outlines were now assuming more concrete shape. He watched, unable to believe in what he was seeing. At first the general outline, non-defined as it was, made him think of a rock ape. But there were no pointed ears above the round skull, no snout on the visage turned in profile toward him.

More and more patches of swamp luminescence were drawn to that glowing figure. What balanced there now, as if walking the treacherous surface of the swampland, was no animal. It was a man, or the semblance of one, a small, thin man—a man he had seen once before, on the terrace of Asaki's mountain fortress.

The thing stood almost complete, its head cocked in what was an attitude of listening.

"Lumbrilo!" Dane identified it, still knowing that the witch doctor could not be standing there listening for them. But, to shake him still farther, the head turned at his cry. Only there were no eyes, no features on the white expanse which should have been a face. And somehow that made the monster more menacing, convincing Dane against sane logic that the thing was spying on them.

"Demon!" That was Nymani; and over his sudden quaver, robbed of all the confidence which had been there only moments earlier, came Asaki's demand:

"What stands there, Medic? Tell us that!"

"A whip to drive us out of hiding, sir. As you know as well as I. If Nymani spied upon them, then they have spied upon us in turn. And this, I think, also answers another question. If there is a canker of trouble on Khatka, then Lumbrilo is close to its root."

"Nymani!" The Chief Ranger's voice was the crack of a lash. "Will you forget again that you are a man, and run crying for shelter against a shaft of light? As this off-world Medic says, Lumbrilo fashions such as that to drive us into our enemies' hands!"

The shadow thing in the swamp moved, putting its foot forward on surface which would not bear the weight of a human body, taking a deliberate step and then another, heading for the concealing brush where the fugitives lay.

"Can you get rid of it, Tau?" Jellico asked in his usual crisp voice. He might have been inquiring about some problem aboard the Queen.

"I'd rather get at the source." There was a grim note in the Medic's reply. "And to do that I want to look at their camp."

"Well enough!" Asaki crept back in the brush.

The ghost of that which was not a man had reached the shore of the island, stood there, its blank head turned toward them. Weird as it was, now that the first shock of sighting it was over, the spacemen could accept and dismiss it as they had not been so able to dismiss the phantom rock ape.

"If that thing was sent to drive us," Dane ventured, "wouldn't we be playing their game by going inland now?"

The Chief Ranger did not pause in his crawl to the left. "I think not. They do not expect us to arrive with our wits about us. Panic-stricken men are easy to pull down. This time Lumbrilo has overreached himself. Had he not played that game with the rock ape, he might have been able to stampede us now."

Though the white thing continued to move inland, it did not change course to fall in behind them on the new route. Whatever it was, it did not possess a mind.

There was a rustling, faint but distinguishable. Then Dane caught Nymani's whisper.

"The one left to watch the inland trail does so no longer. We need not fear an alarm from him. Also, here is another blaster for our use."

Away from the open by the swamp, the gloom was deeper. Dane was guided only by the noises of the less-experienced Jellico and Tau made in their progress.

They edged down into a small cut, floored with reeds and mud, where some of the moisture from the soggy land about them gathered into a half pool. Straight through this swale the Khatkans set course.

The drum beat grew louder. Now there was a glow against the dark—fire ahead? Dane squirmed forward and at last gained a vantage point from which to survey the poachers' camp.

There were shelters erected there, three of them, but they were mainly roofs of leaves and branches. In two of them were stored bales of hides sewn into plastic cloth, ready to ship. Before the third hut lounged four off-worlders. And Nymani was very right; one of them wore ship's uniform.

To the right of the fire was a ring of natives and another man, slightly apart, who beat the drum. But of the witch doctor there was no sign. And Dane, thinking of that mist-born thing at the swamp's edge, shivered. He could believe Tau's explanation of the drug which produced hallucinations back on the mountain side. But how that likeness fashioned of phosphorescence had been sent by an absent man to hunt his enemies was a eerie puzzle.

"Lumbrilo is not here." Nymani's thoughts must have been moving along the same path.

Dane could hear movements in the dark beside him.

"There's a long-distance com unit in that third hut," Tau observed.

"So I see," Jellico snapped. "Could you reach your men over the mountain with that, sir?"

"I do not know. But if Lumbrilo is not here, how can he make his image walk the night?" the Chief Ranger demanded impatiently.

"We shall see. If Lumbrilo is not here—he shall come." And the promise in Tau's tone was sure. "Those off-worlders will have to be out of action first. And with that walking thing sent to drive us in, they must be waiting for us."

"If they have sentries out, I will silence them!" promised Nymani.

"You have a plan?" Asaki's wide shoulders and upheld head showed for an instant against the light from the camp.

"You want Lumbrilo," Tau replied. "Very well, sir, I believe I can give him to you, and in the doing discredit him with your Khatkans. But not with the off-worlders free to move."

The program was not going to be easy, Dane decided. Every one of the poachers was armed with a Patrol blaster of the latest type, and a small part of his mind speculated as to what would be the result of that information conveyed to official quarters. Free Traders and Patrolmen did not always see eye-to-eye over the proper action to be taken on the galactic frontier. The Queen's crew had had one such brush with authority in the immediate past. But each realized that the other had an important role in the general scheme of things, and if it came to a clash between the law and outlaws, Free Traders fought beside the Patrol.

"Why not give them what they expect—with reservations?" inquired Jellico. "They've set us up to be stampeded into camp, flying ahead of that tame ghost of theirs. Suppose we do stampede—after Nymani has removed any sentries—stampede so well we sweep right over them? I want to get at that com unit."

"You don't think they'll just mow us down as we come in?"

"You delivered a blow to Lumbrilo's pride; he won't be satisfied with just your burning," the captain answered Tau, "not if I'm any judge of character. And we'd furnish hostages of a sort—especially the Chief Ranger. No, if they had wanted to kill us they would have shot us off those islands when we came here. There would have been no playing around with ghosts and goblins."

"There is reason in your words. And it is true they would like to have me, those outlaws down there," Asaki commented. "I am of the Magawaya and we have pressed always for stronger security methods to be used against such as they. But I do not see how we can take the camp."

"We won't go in from the front—as they expect us to do. But a try from the north, getting at the off-worlders first.... Three men causing enough disturbance to cover operations of the other two...."

"So?" There was a moment of silence as the Chief Ranger evaluated that. Then he added a few comments of his own.

"That off-worlder who wears spaceman's clothing, his weapon is not drawn, though the others are ready. But I believe that you are right in thinking they expect to be warned by sentries. Those we can see to. Suppose then, Captain, you and I play the fear-crazed men running from demons. Nymani will cover us from the dark and your two men—"

Tau spoke up, "Give me leave to flush out our other quarry, sir. I believe I can keep him occupied. Dane, you'll take the drum."

"Drum?" With his mind on blasters, it was startling to be offered a noise-maker.

"It's your business to get that drum. And when you get it I want you to beat out 'Terra Bound.' You certainly can play that, can't you?"

"I don't understand," Dane began and then swallowed the rest of his protest, knowing that Tau was not going to explain why he needed to have the hackneyed popular song of the spaceways played in a Khatkan swamp. As a Free Trader he had had quite a few odd jobs handed him during the past couple of years, but this was the first time he had been ordered to serve as a musician.

They waited for Nymani through dragging minutes. Surely those in the camp would expect their arrival soon now? Dane's fire ray was in his hand as he measured the distance to the drummer's stand.

"It is done," Nymani whispered from the darkness behind them. Jellico and the Chief Ranger moved to the left; Tau crept to the right and Dane pushed level with the medic.

"When they move," Tau's lips were beside his ear, "jump for that drum. I don't care how you get it, but get it and keep it!"

"Yes, sir!"

There was a wailing cry from the north, a howl of witless fear. The singers stopped in mid-note, the drummer paused, his hand uplifted. Dane darted forward in a plunge which carried him to that man. The Khatkan did not have time to rise from his knees as the barrel of the fire rod struck his head, sending him spinning. Then the drum was cradled in the spaceman's arm, close to his chest, his weapon aimed across it at the startled natives.

The crackle of blaster fire, the shrill whine of needlers in action, raised a bedlam from the other end of the camp. Backing up a little, Dane went down on one knee, his weapon ready to sweep over the bewildered natives, the drum resting on the earth against his body. Keeping the fire rod steady, his left hand went to work, not in the muted cadence the Khatkan drummer had chosen, but in hard and vigorous thumps which rolled across the clamor of the fight. There was no forgetting the beat of "Terra Bound" and he delivered it with force, so that the familiar da-dah-da-da droned loud enough to awaken the whole camp.

Dane's move appeared to completely baffle the Khatkan outlaws. They stared at him, the whites of their eyes doubly noticeable in their dark faces, their mouths a little agape. As usual the unexpected had driven them off guard. He dared not look away from that gathering to see how the fight at the other end of the camp was progressing. But he did see Tau's advance.

The medic came into the light of the fire, not with his ordinary loose-limbed spaceman's stride, but mincingly, with a dancing step, and he was singing to the drum beat of "Terra Bound." Dane could not understand the words, but he knew that they patterned in and out of the drum beats, weaving a net between singer and listeners as Lumbrilo had woven his net on the mountain terrace.

Tau had them! Had every one of the native outlaws ensnared, so that Dane rested his weapon across his knee and took up the lower beat with the fingers of his right hand as well.

Da-dah-da-da.... The innocuous repetitive refrain of the original song which had been repeating itself in his mind faded, and somehow he caught the menace in the new words Tau was mouthing.

Twice the medic shuffled about a circle of his own making. Then he stooped, took a hunting knife from the belt of the nearest Khatkan and held it point out toward the dark east. Dane would not have believed the medic knew the drill he now displayed, for with no opponent save the dancing firelight he fought a knife duel, feinting, striking, twisting, retreating, attacking, all in time to the beat of the drum Dane was no longer conscious of playing. And as he strove it was very easy to picture another fighting against him. So that when the knife came up in a vicious thrust which was the finish of his last attack, Dane stared stupidly at the ground, half expecting to see a body lying there.

Once more Tau ceremoniously saluted with his blade to the east. Then he laid it on the ground and stood astride its gleaming length.

"Lumbrilo!" His confident voice arose above the call of the drum. "Lumbrilo—I am waiting."

VIII

Vaguely aware that the clamor at the other end of the camp had died away, Dane muted the sound of his drum. Over its round top he could watch the Khatkan outlaws; their heads bobbed and swayed in time to the beat of his fingers. He, too, could feel the pull of Tau's voice. But what would come in answer? That shadowy thing which had been loosed to drive them here? Or the man himself?

To Dane, the ruddy light of the fire dimmed, yet there was no actual dying of those flames which coiled and thrust around the wood. And the acrid scent of burning was thick. How much of what followed was real, how much the product of his tense nerves, Dane was never afterwards able to tell. In fact, whether all the witnesses there saw the same sights could be questioned. Did each man, Khatkan and off-worlder, see only what his particular set of emotions and memories dictated?

Something swept in from the east, something which was not as tangible as the creature born of swamp mist. Rather it came as an unseen menace to the fire, and all that fire signifies to human kind—security, comradeship, a weapon against the age-old forces of the dangerous night. Was that threat, too, only in their minds? Or had Lumbrilo some power to so shape his hatred?

The unseen was cold; it sapped a man's strength, bit at his brain, weighted his hands and feet, weakened him. It strove to soften him into clay another could remold. Nothingness, darkness, all that was opposed to life and warmth and reality, arose in the night, gathered together against them.

Yet still Tau fronted that invisible wave, his head high. And between his sturdily planted feet the knife gleamed bright with a radiance of its own.

"Ahhh—" Tau's voice curled out, to pierce that creeping menace. Then he was singing again, the cadence of his unknown words rising a little above the pattern wrought by the drum.

Dane forced his heavy hands to continue the beat, his wrists to rise and fall in defiance of that which crept to eat their strength and make them less then men.

"Lumbrilo! I, Tau, of another star, another sky, another world, bid you come forth and range your power against mine!" Now there was a sharper note in that demand, the snap of an order.

He was answered by another wave of the black negation—stronger, rolling up to smash them down, as a wave in the heavy surf of a wild ocean pounds its force against the beach. This time Dane thought he could see that dark mass. He tore his eyes away before it took on substance, concentrating on the movements of his hands against the drum head, refusing to believe that hammer of power was rising to flatten them all. He had heard Tau describe such things in the past. But told in familiar quarters on board the Queen, such experiences were only stories. Here was danger unleashed. Yet the medic stood unbowed as the wave broke upon him in full.

And, advancing under the crest of that lick of destruction, came its controller. This was no ghost drawn from the materials of the swamp; this was a man, walking quietly, his hands as empty as Tau's, yet grasping weapons none of them could see.

In the firelight, as the wave receded sullenly, men moaned, lay face down upon the ground, beat their hands feebly against the earth. But, as Lumbrilo came on from the shadows, one of them got to his hands and knees, moving with small tortured jerks. He crawled toward Tau, his head lolling on his shoulders as the head of the dead rock ape had done. Dane patted the drum with one hand while, with the other, he groped for his fire ray. He tried to shout in warning and found that he could not utter a sound.

Tau's arm moved, raised from his side, made a circling motion.

The creeping man, his eyes rolled up in his head until only the whites gleamed blindly in the limited light, followed that gesture. He drew level with the medic, passed beyond toward Lumbrilo, whining as a hound prevented from obeying his master might lament.

"So be it, Lumbrilo," Tau said. "This is between you and me. Or do you not dare to risk your power against mine? Is Lumbrilo so weak a one that he must send another to do his will?"

Raising both hands again the medic brought them down, curling inward, until he stooped and touched them to the ground. When he straightened once again the knife was in his grasp and he tossed it behind him.

The smoke from the fire swirled out in a long tongue, coiled about Lumbrilo and was gone. A black and white beast stood where the man had been, its tufted tail lashing, its muzzle a mask of snarling hate and blood lust.

But Tau met that transformation with laughter which was like the lash of a whip.

"We both be men, you and I, Lumbrilo. Meet me as a man and keep those trickeries for those who have not the clear sight. A child plays as a child, so—" Tau's voice came in a rumble, but Tau was gone. The huge, hairy thing which swayed in his place turned a gorilla's beast visage to his enemy. For a breathless moment Terran ape confronted Khatkan lion. Then the spaceman was himself again. "The time for games is over, man of Khatka. You have tried to hunt us to our deaths, have you not? Therefore death shall be the portion of the loser now."

Lion vanished, man stood watching, alertly, as swordsman might face swordsman with a blood feud lying on their blades. To Dane's eyes the Khatkan made no move. Yet the fire leaped high, as if freshly fed, and flames burst from the wood, flew into the air, red and perilous birds, darting at Tau until they outlined him from the ground under his boots to an arch over his head. They united and spun faster until Dane, watching with dazzled eyes, saw the wheel become a blur of light, hiding Tau within its fiery core. His own wrists ached with the strain of his drumming as he lifted one hand and tried to shield his sight from the glare of that pillar of fire.

Lumbrilo was chanting—a heavy blast of words. Dane stiffened; his traitorous hands were falling into the rhythm of that other song! Straightaway he raised both from the drum head, brought them down in a discordinate series of thumps which bore no relation to either the song Tau wanted or that which Lumbrilo was now crooning. Thump—thump—thump—Dane beat it out frantically, belaboring the drum head as he wanted to sink his fists home on the body of the Khatkan witch doctor.

The pillar of fire swayed, fluttered as if a wind drove it—and was gone. Tau, unmarked, smiled.

"Fire!" He pointed his fingers at Lumbrilo. "Would you try earth, and water, and air also, wizard? Call hither your whirlwind, up your flood, summon the land to quake. None of those shall bring me down!"

Shapes came flooding out of the night, some monstrous, some human, streaming past Lumbrilo to crowd into the circle of firelight. Some Dane thought he knew, some were strangers. Men wearing space uniforms, or the dress of other worlds, women—they strode, wept, mingled with the monsters to laugh, curse, threaten.

Dane guessed that Lumbrilo sent now against the Terran the harvest of the medic's own memories. He shut his eyes against this enforced intrusion upon another's past, but not before he saw Tau's face, strained, fined to the well-shaped bones beneath the thin flesh, holding still a twisted smile as he met each memory, accepted the pain it held for him, and set it aside unshaken.

"This, too, has no power any longer, man who walks in the dark."

Dane opened his eyes. Those crowding wraiths were fading, losing substance. Lumbrilo crouched, his lips drawn back from his teeth, his hatred plain to read.

"I am not clay to be molded by your hands, Lumbrilo. And now I say that the time has come to call an end—"

Tau raised his hands slowly once again, holding them away from his body, palms pointing earthward. And beneath them, on either side of the spaceman, two black shadows gathered on the surface of the ground.

"You have fettered yourself with your own bounds. As you have been the hunter, so shall you now be the hunted."

Those shadows were growing as plants might issue from the packed soil of the camping ground. When his hands were shoulder high, Tau held them steady. Now on either side of his tautly held body crouched one of the black-and-white lions with which Lumbrilo had identified his own brand of magic throughout the year.

Lumbrilo's "lion" had been larger than life, more intelligent, more dangerous, subtly different from the normal animal it counterfeited. So now were these. And both of them raised their heads to gaze intently into the medic's face.

"Hunt well, brothers in fur," he said slowly, almost caressingly. "Him whom you hunt shall grant you sport in the going."

"Stop it!" A man leaped from the shadows behind the witch doctor. Firelight made plain his off-world dress, and he swung up a blaster, aiming at the nearest of the waiting beasts. That flash struck true, but it neither killed nor even singed the fine fur of the animal's pelt.

As the blaster's aim was swung from beast to man, Dane fired first. His ray brought a scream from the other, who dropped his weapon from a badly seared hand to reel back, cursing.

Tau waved his hands gently. The great animal heads turned obediently, until the red eyes were set on Lumbrilo. Facing them, the witch doctor straightened, spat out his hate at the medic:

"I do not run to be hunted, devil man!"

"I think you do, Lumbrilo. For you must taste fear now as you have made other men drink of it, so that it fills your blood and races through your body, clouds your mind to make of you less than a man. You have hunted out those who doubted your power, who stood in your chosen path, whom you wanted removed from the earth of Khatka. Do you doubt that they wait in the last dark for you now, ready to greet you, witch doctor? What they have known, you shall also know. This night you have shown me all that lies in my past that is weak, that was evil, that I may regret or find sorrow for. So shall you also remember through the few hours left you. Aye, you shall run, Lumbrilo!"

As he spoke, Tau approached the other, the two black-and-white hunters pacing beside him. Now he stooped and caught up a pinch of soil and spat upon it three times. Then he threw the tiny clod of earth at the witch doctor. It struck Lumbrilo just above the heart and the man reeled under what might have been a murderous blow.

The Khatkan broke then, completely. With a wailing cry he whirled and ran, crashing into the brush as one who runs blindly and without hope. Behind him the two beasts leaped noiselessly together and all three were gone.

Tau swayed, put his hand to his head. Dane kicked away the drum, arose from his cramped position stiffly to go to him. But the medic was not yet done. He returned to stand over the prostrate native hunters and he clapped his hands sharply.

"You are men, and you shall act as men henceforth. That which was, is no longer. Stand free, for the dark power follows him who misused it, and fear no longer eats from your basins, drinks from your cups, or lies beside you on the sleep mats."

"Tau!" Jellico's shout reached them over the cries of the rousing Khatkans. But Dane was there first, catching the medic before he slumped to the ground; but he was dragged with that dead weight until he sat with the medic's head on his shoulder, the other's body resting heavily against him. For one horror-filled moment Dane feared that he did indeed hold a dead man, that one of the outlaw Hunters must have struck a last blow for his discredited leader. Then Tau sighed and began to breathe deeply. Dane glanced up, amazed, at the captain.

"He's asleep!"

Jellico knelt and his hand went to test heart beat, then to touch the medic's worn and dirty face. "Best thing for him," he said briskly. "He's had it."

It took some time to get the facts of their triumph sorted out. Two of the off-worlder poachers were dead. The other and the spaceman were prisoners, while Nymani rounded up in addition the man Dane had burned to save Tau. When the younger spaceman returned from making the medic comfortable in the shelter, he found Asaki and Jellico holding an impromptu court of inquiry.

The dazed native Hunters had been expertly looped together by Nymani and, a little apart from them, the off-worlders were under examination.

"An I-C man, eh?" Jellico, smoothing a mud-spattered chin with a grimed hand, regarded the latest arrival measuringly. "Trying to run in and break a Combine charter, were you? You'd better spill the facts; your own head office will disown you, you ought to

94

know that. They never back any failures in these undercover deals."

"I want medical attention," snapped the other, cradling his seared hand to his chest. "Or do you plan to turn me over to these savages?"

"Seeing as how you tried to blast our medic," replied the captain with a grin which was close to shark-like, "he may not feel much like patching up those fingers of yours. Stick 'em in where they have no business, and they're apt to get burned. At any rate he's not going to look at 'em until he's had a chance to rest. I'll give you first aid. And while I'm working we'll talk. I-C going into the poaching trade now? That news is going to please Combine; they have no use for you boys anyway."

His answer was lurid and uninformative. But the uniform tunic the other wore could not be so easily explained away. Dane, worn out, stretched his aching length on a pile of mats and lost all interest in the argument.

Two days later they stood once more on the same terrace where Lumbrilo had wrought his magic and met his first defeat. This time no lightning played along the mountain ridges and the blaze of the sun was so bright and clear that one could hardly believe in the fantastic happenings of that swamp clearing where men had fought with weapons not made by hands. The three from the Queen moved away from the parapet to meet the Chief Ranger as he came down the stairs.

"A messenger has just arrived. The hunter was hunted indeed, and his going was witnessed by many—though they did not see those which hunted him. Lumbrilo is dead; he came to his end by the Great River."

Jellico started. "But that is almost fifty miles from the swamp, on this side of the mountain!"

"He was hunted and he fled—as you promised," Asaki said to Tau. "You made strong magic, off-world man."

The medic shook his head slowly. "I but turned his own methods against him. Because he believed in his power, that same power, reflected back, broke him. Had I been facing one who did not believe...." He shrugged. "Our first meeting set the pattern. From that moment he feared a little that I could match him, and his uncertainty pierced a hole in his armor."

"Why on earth did you want 'Terra Bound?'" burst out Dane, still seeking an explanation for that one small mystery among the others.

Tau chuckled. "In the first place, that blasted tune has haunted us all for so long that I knew its rhythm was probably the one you could keep to without hardly knowing that you were beating it out. And, in the second place, its alien pattern was a part of our particular background, to counteract Lumbrilo's native Khatkan music, which was certainly a big factor in his stage setting. He must have believed that we would not find out about the drugged water and so would be prepared for any fantasy he cared to produce. When they saw us coming out over the swamp they counted us easy takings. His practice had always been with Khatkans, and he judged us by their reactions to stimuli he knew well how to use. So he failed...."

Asaki smiled. "Which was good for Khatka but ill for Lumbrilo and those using him to make mischief here. The poacher and the outlaw Hunters will meet with our justice, which I do not believe they will relish. But the other two, the spaceman and the company agent, are to be sent to Xecho to face Combine authorities. It is my thought that those will not accept kindly the meddling of another company in their territory."

Jellico grunted. "Kindness and Combine are widely separated in such matters. But we can now take passage on the same ship as your prisoners—"

"But, my friend, you have not yet seen the preserve. I assure you that this time there shall be no trouble. We have several days yet before you must return to your ship—"

The captain of the Queen held up his hand. "Nothing would give me greater pleasure than to inspect the Zoboru preserve, sir—next year. As it is, my holiday is over and the Queen is waiting for us on Xecho. Also, permit me to send you some tapes dealing with the newest types of flitters—guaranteed against flight failures."

"Yes, guaranteed," Tau added guilelessly, "not to break down, lose course, or otherwise disrupt a pleasant excursion."

The Chief Ranger threw back his head and his deep-chested laughter was echoed from the heights above them. "Very well, Captain. Your mail run will bring you back to Xecho at intervals. Meanwhile I shall study your sales tapes concerning the non-expendable flitters. But you shall visit Zoboru—and pleasantly, very pleasantly, I assure you, Medic Tau!"

"I wonder," Tau muttered and Dane heard. "Just now the quiet of deep space is a far, far more entrancing proposition!"

THE GFTS OF ASTI

She was the guardian of the worlds, but HER world was dead.

Even here, on the black terrace before the forgotten mountain retreat of Asti, it was possible to smell the dank stench of burning Memphir, to imagine that the dawn wind bore upward from the pillaged city the faint tortured cries of those whom the barbarians of Klem hunted to their prolonged death. Indeed it was time to leave—

Varta, last of the virgin Maidens of Asti, shivered. The scaled and wattled creature who crouched beside her thigh turned his reptilian head so that golden eyes met the aquamarine ones set slantingly at a faintly provocative angle in her smooth ivory face.

"We go—?"

She nodded in answer to that unvoiced question Lur had sent into her brain, and turned toward the dark cavern which was the mouth of Asti's last dwelling place. Once, more than a thousand years before when the walls of Memphir were young, Asti had lived among men below. But in the richness and softness which was trading Memphir, empire of empires, Asti found no place. So He and those who served Him had withdrawn to this mountain outcrop. And she, Varta, was the last, the very last to bow knee at Asti's shrine and raise her voice in the dawn hymn—for Lur, as were all his race, was mute.

98

Even the loot of Memphir would not sate the shaggy headed warriors who had stormed her gates this day. The stairway to Asti's Temple was plain enough to see and there would be those to essay the steep climb hoping to find a treasure which did not exist. For Asti was an austere God, delighting in plain walls and bare altars. His last priest had lain in the grave niches these three years, there would be none to hold that gate against intruders.

Varta passed between tall, uncarved pillars, Lur padding beside her, his spine mane erect, the talons on his forefeet clicking on the stone in steady rhythm. So they came into the innermost shrine of Asti and there Varta made graceful obeisance to the great cowled and robed figure which sat enthroned, its hidden eyes focused upon its own outstretched hand.

And above the flattened palm of that wide hand hung suspended in space the round orange-red sun ball which was twin to the sun that lighted Erb. Around the miniature sun swung in their orbits the four worlds of the system, each obeying the laws of space, even as did the planets they represented.

"Memphir has fallen," Varta's voice sounded rusty in her own ears. She had spoken so seldom during the last lonely months. "Evil has risen to overwhelm our world, even as it was prophesied in Your Revelations, O, Ruler of Worlds and Maker of Destiny. Therefore, obeying the order given of old, I would depart from this, Thy house. Suffer me now to fulfill the Law—"

Three times she prostrated her slim body on the stones at the foot of Asti's judgment chair. Then she arose and, with the confidence of a child in its father, she laid her hand palm upward upon the outstretched hand of Asti. Beneath her flesh the stone was not cold and hard, but seemed to have an inner heat, even as might a

99

human hand. For a long moment she stood so and then she raised her hand slowly, carefully, as if within its slight hollow she cupped something precious.

And, as she drew her hand away from the grasp of Asti, the tiny sun and its planets followed, spinning now above her palm as they had above the statue's. But out of the cowled figure some virtue had departed with the going of the miniature solar system; it was now but a carving of stone. And Varta did not look at it again as she passed behind its bulk to seek a certain place in the temple wall, known to her from much reading of the old records.

Having found the stone she sought, she moved her hand in a certain pattern before it so that the faint radiance streaming from the tiny sun, gleamed on the grayness of the wall. There was a grating, as from metal long unused, and a block fell back, opening a narrow door to them.

Before she stepped within, the priestess lifted her hand above her head and when she withdrew it, the sun and planets remained to form a diadem just above the intricate braiding of her dull red hair. As she moved into the secret way, the five orbs swung with her, and in the darkness there the sun glowed richly, sending out a light to guide their feet.

They were at the top of a stairway and the hollow clang of the stone as it moved back into place behind them echoed through a gulf which seemed endless. But that too was as the chronicles had said and Varta knew no fear.

How long they journeyed down into the maw of the mountain and, beyond that, into the womb of Erb itself, Varta never knew. But, when feet were weary and she knew the bite of real hunger, they came into a passageway which ended in a room hollowed of solid rock. And there, preserved in the chest in which men born in the youth of Memphir had laid them, Varta found that which would keep her safe on the path she must take. She put aside the fine silks, the jeweled cincture, which had been the badge of Asti's service and drew on over her naked body a suit of scaled skin, gemmed and glistening in the rays of the small sun. There was a hood to cover the entire head, taloned gloves for the hands, webbed, clawed coverings for the feet—as if the skin of a giant, man-like lizard had been tanned and fashioned into this suit. And Varta suspected that that might be so—the world of Erb had not always been held by the human-kind alone.

There were supplies here too, lying untouched in ageless containers within a lizard-skin pouch. Varta touched her tongue without fear to a powdered restorative, sharing it with Lur, whose own mailed skin would protect him through the dangers to come.

She folded the regalia she had stripped off and laid it in the chest, smoothing it regretfully before she dropped the lid upon its shimmering color. Never again would Asti's servant wear the soft stuff of His Livery. But she was resolute enough when she picked up the food pouch and strode forward, passing out of the robing chamber into a narrow way which was a natural fault in the rock unsmoothed by the tools of man.

But when this rocky road ended upon the lip of a gorge, Varta hesitated, plucking at the throat latch of her hood-like helmet. Through the unclouded crystal of its eye-holes she could see the sprouts of yellow vapor which puffed from crannies in the rock wall down which she must climb. If the records of the Temple spoke true, these curls of gas were death to all lunged creatures of the upper world. She could only trust that the cunning of the scaled hood would not fail her.

The long talons fitted to the finger tips of the gloves, the claws of the webbed foot coverings clamped fast to every hand and foot hold, but the way down was long and she caught a message of weariness from Lur before they reached the piled rocks at the foot of the cliff. The puffs of steamy gas had become a fog through which they groped their way slowly, following a trace of path along the base of the cliff.

Time did not exist in the underworld of Erb. Varta did not know whether it was still today, or whether she had passed into tomorrow when they came to a cross roads. She felt Lur press against her, forcing her back against a rock.

"There is a thing coming—" his message was clear.

And in a moment she too saw a dark hulk nosing through the vapor. It moved slowly, seeming to balance at each step as if travel was a painful act. But it bore steadily to the meeting of the two paths.

"It is no enemy—" But she did not need that reassurance from Lur. Unearthly as the thing looked it had no menace.

With a last twist of ungainly body the creature squatted on a rock and clawed the clumsy covering it wore about its bone-thin shoulders and domed-skull head. The visage it revealed was long and gray, with dark pits for eyes and a gaping, fang-studded, lipless mouth.

"Who are you who dare to tread the forgotten ways and rouse from slumber the Guardian of the Chasms?"

The question was a shrill whine in her brain, her hands half arose to cover her ears —

"I am Varta, Maiden of Asti. Memphir has fallen to the barbarians of the Outer Lands and now I go, as Asti once ordered —."

The Guardian considered her answer gravely. In one skeleton claw it fumbled a rod and with this it now traced certain symbols in the dust before Varta's webbed feet. When it had done, the girl stooped and altered two of the lines with a swift stroke from one of her talons. The creature of the Chasm nodded its misshapen head.

"Asti does not rule here. But long, and long, and long ago there was a pact made with us in His Name. Pass free from us, woman of the Light. There are two paths before you —."

The Guardian paused for so long that Varta dared to prompt it.

"Where do they lead, Guardian of the Dark?"

"This will take you down into my country," it jerked the rod to the right. "And that way is death for creatures from the surface world. The other — in our old legends it is said to bring a traveler out into the upper world. Of the truth of that I have no proof."

"But that one I must take," she made slight obeisance to the huddle of bones and dank cloak on the rock and it inclined its head in grave courtesy.

With Lur pushing a little ahead, she took the road which ran straight into the flume-veiled darkness. Nor did she turn to look again at the Thing from the Chasm world.

They began to climb again, across slimed rock where there were evil trails of other things which lived in this haunted darkness. But the sun of Asti lighted their way and perhaps some virtue in the rays from it kept away the makers of such trails.

When they pulled themselves up onto a wide ledge the talons on Varta's gloves were worn to splintered stubs and there was a bright girdle of pain about her aching body. Lur lay panting beside her, his red-forked tongue protruding from his foam ringed mouth.

"We walk again the ways of men," Lur was the first to note the tool marks on the stone where they lay. "By the Will of Asti, we may win out of this maze after all."

Since there were no signs of the deadly steam Varta dared to push off her hood and share with her companion the sustaining power she carried in her pouch. There was a freshness to the air they breathed, damp and cold though it was, which hinted of the upper world.

The ledge sloped upwards, at a steep angle at first, and then more gently. Lur slipped past her and thrust head and shoulders through a break in the rock. Grasping his neck spines she allowed him to pull her through that narrow slit into the soft blackness of a surface night. They tumbled down together, Varta's head pillowed on Lur's smooth side, and so slept as the sun and worlds of Asti whirled protectingly above them.

A whir of wings in the air above her head awakened Varta. One of the small, jewel bright flying lizard creatures of the deep jungle poised and dipped to investigate more closely the worlds of Asti. But at Varta's upflung arm it uttered a rasping cry and planed down into the mass of vegetation below. By the glint of sunlight on the stone around them the day was already well advanced. Varta tugged at Lur's mane until he roused.

There was a regularity to the rocks piled about their sleeping place which hinted that they had lain among the ruins left by man. But of this side of the mountains both were ignorant, for Memphir's rule had not run here.

"Many dead things in times past," Lur's scarlet nostril pits were extended to their widest. "But that was long ago. This land is no longer held by men."

Varta laughed cheerfully. "If here there are no men, then there will rise no barbarian hordes to dispute our rule. Asti has led us to safety. Let us see more of the land He gives us."

There was a road leading down from the ruins, a road still to be followed in spite of the lash of landslip and the crack of time. And it brought them into a cup of green fertility where the lavishness of Asti's sowing was unchecked by man. Varta seized eagerly upon globes of blood red fruit which she recognized as delicacies which had been cultivated in the Temple gardens, while Lur went hunting into the fringes of the jungle, there dining on prey so easily caught as to be judged devoid of fear.

The jungle choked highway curved and they were suddenly fronted by a desert of sere desolation, a desert floored by glassy slag which sent back the sun beams in a furnace glare. Varta shaded her eyes and tried to see the end of this, but, if there was a distant rim of green beyond, the heat distortions in the air concealed it.

Lur put out a front paw to test the slag but withdrew it instantly.

"It cooks the flesh, we can not walk here," was his verdict.

Varta pointed with her chin to the left where, some distance away, the mountain wall paralleled their course.

"Then let us keep to the jungle over there and see if it does not bring around to the far side. But what made this—?" She leaned out over the glassy stuff, not daring to touch the slick surface.

"War." Lur's tongue shot out to impale a questing beetle. "These forgotten people fought with fearsome weapons."

"But what weapon could do this? Memphir knew not such—."

"Memphir was old. But mayhap there were those who raised cities on Erb before the first hut of Memphir squatted on tidal mud. Men forget knowledge in time. Even in Memphir the lords of the last days forgot the wisdom of their earlier sages—they fell before the barbarians easily enough."

"If ever men had wisdom to produce this—it was not of Asti's giving," she edged away from the glare. "Let us go."

But now they had to fight their way through jungle and it was hard—until they reached a ridge of rock running out from the mountain as a tongue thrust into the blasted valley. And along this they picked their slow way.

"There is water near—," Lur's thought answered the girl's desire. She licked dry lips longingly. "This way—," her companion's sudden turn was to the left and Varta was quick to follow him down a slide of rock.

Lur's instinct was right, as it ever was. There was water before them, a small lake of it. But even as he dipped his fanged muzzle toward that inviting surface, Lur's spined head jerked erect again. Varta snatched back the hand she had put out, staring at Lur's strange actions. His nostrils expanded to their widest, his long neck outstretched, he was swinging his head back and forth across the limpid shallows.

"What is it—?"

"This is no water such as we know," the scaled one answered flatly. "It has life within it."

Varta laughed. "Fish, water snakes, your own distant kin, Lur. It is the scent of them which you catch—"

"No. It is the water itself which lives—and yet does not live—" His thought trailed away from her as he struggled with some problem. No human brain could follow his unless he willed it so.

Varta squatted back on her heels and began to look at the water and then at the banks with more care. For the first time she noted the odd patches of brilliant color which floated just below the surface of the liquid. Blue, green, yellow, crimson, they drifted slowly with the tiny waves which lapped the shore. But they were not alive, she was almost sure of that, they appeared more a part of the water itself.

Watching the voyage of one patch of green she caught sight of the branch. It was a drooping shoot of the turbi, the same tree vine which produced the fruit she had relished less than an hour before. Above the water dangled a cluster of the fruit, dead ripe with the sweet pulp stretching its skin. But below the surface of the water—

Varta's breath hissed between her teeth and Lur's head snapped around as he caught her thought.

The branch below the water bore a perfect circle of green flowers close to its tip, the flowers which the turbi had borne naturally seven months before and which should long ago have turned into just such sweetness as hung above.

With Lur at her heels the girl edged around to pull cautiously at the branch. It yielded at once to her touch, swinging its tip out of the lake. She sniffed—there was a languid perfume in the air, the perfume of the blooming turbi. She examined the flowers closely, to all appearances they were perfect and natural.

"It preserves," Lur settled back on his haunches and waved one front paw at the quiet water. "What goes into it remains as it was just at the moment of entrance."

"But if this is seven months old—"

"It may be seven years old," corrected Lur. "How can you tell when that branch first dipped into the lake? Yet the flowers do not fade even when withdrawn from the water. This is indeed a mystery!"

"Of which I would know more!" Varta dropped the turbi and started on around the edge of the lake.

Twice more they found similar evidence of preservation in flower or leaf, wherever it was covered by the opaline water.

The lake itself was a long and narrow slash with one end cutting into the desert of glass while the other wet the foot of the mountain. And it was there, on the slope of the mountain that they found the greatest wonder of all, Lur scenting it before they sighted the remains among the stones.

"Man made," he cautioned, "but very, very old."

And truly the wreckage they came upon must have been old, perhaps even older than Memphir. For the part which rested above the water was almost gone, rusty red stains on the rocks outlining where it had lain. But under water was a smooth silver hull, shining and untouched by the years. Varta laid her hand upon a ruddy scrap between two rocks and it became a drift of powdery dust. And yet—there a few feet below was strong metal!

Lur padded along the scrap of shore surveying the thing.

"It was a machine in which men traveled," his thoughts arose to her. "But they were not as the men of Memphir. Perhaps not even as the sons of Erb—"

"Not as the sons of Erb!" her astonishment broke into open speech.

Lur's neck twisted as he looked up at her. "Did the men of Erb, even in the old chronicles fight with weapons such as would make a desert of glass? There are other worlds than Erb, mayhap this strange thing was a sky ship from such a world. All things are possible by the Will of Asti."

Varta nodded. "All things are possible by the Will of Asti," she repeated. "But, Lur," her eyes were round with wonder, "perhaps it is Asti's Will which brought us here to find this marvel! Perhaps He has some use for us and it!"

"At least we may discover what lies within it," Lur had his own share of curiosity.

"How? The two of us can not draw that out of the water!"

"No, but we can enter into it!"

Varta fingered the folds of the hood on her shoulders. She knew what Lur meant, the suit which had protected her in the underworld was impervious to everything outside its surface—or to every substance its makers knew—just as Lur's own hide made his flesh impenetrable. But the fashioners of her suit had probably never known of the living lake and what if she had no defense against the strange properties of the water?

She leaned back against a rock. Overhead the worlds and sun of Asti still traveled their appointed paths. The worlds of Asti! If it was His Will which had brought them here, then Asti's power would wrap her round with safety. By His Will she had come out of Memphir over ways no human of Erb had ever trod before. Could she doubt that His Protection was with her now?

It took only a moment to make secure the webbed shoes, to pull on and fasten the hood, to tighten the buckles of her gloves. Then she crept forward, shuddering as the water rose about her ankles. But Lur pushed on before her, his head disappearing fearlessly under the surface as he crawled through the jagged opening in the ship below.

Smashed engines which had no meaning in her eyes occupied most of the broken section of the wreck. None of the metal showed any deterioration beyond that which had occurred at the time of the crash. Under her exploring hands it was firm and whole.

Lur was pulling at a small door half hidden by a mass of twisted wires and plates and, just as Varta crawled around this obstacle to join him, the barrier gave way allowing them to squeeze through into what had once been the living quarters of the ship.

Varta recognized seats, a table, and other bits of strictly utilitarian furniture. But of those who had once been at home there, there remained no trace. Lur, having given one glance to the furnishings, was prowling about the far end of the cabin uncertainly, and now he voiced his uneasiness.

"There is something beyond, something which once had life—"

Varta crowded up to him. To her eyes the wall seemed without line of an opening, and yet Lur was running his broad front paws over it carefully, now and then throwing his weight against the smooth surface.

"There is no door—" she pointed out doubtfully.

"No door—ah—here—" Lur unsheathed formidable fighting claws to their full length for perhaps the first time in his temple-sheltered life, and endeavored to work them into a small crevice. The muscles of his forelegs and quarters stood out in sharp relief under his scales, his fangs were bare as his lips snapped back with effort.

Something gave, a thin black line appeared to mark the edges of a door. Then time, or Lur's strength, broke the ancient locking mechanism. The door gave so suddenly that they were both sent hurtling backward and Lur's breath burst from him in a huge bubble.

The sealed compartment was hardly more than a cupboard but it was full. Spread-eagled against the wall was a four-limbed

111

creature whose form was so smothered in a bulky suit that Varta could only guess that it was akin in shape to her own. Hoops of metal locked it firmly to the wall, but the head had fallen forward so that the face plate in the helmet was hidden.

Slowly the girl breasted the water which filled the cabin and reached her hands toward the bowed helmet of the prisoner. Gingerly, her blunted talons scraping across metal, she pulled it up to her eye-level.

The eyes of that which stood within the suit were closed, as if in sleep, but there was a warm, healthy tint to the bronze skin, so different in shade to her own pallid coloring. For the rest, the prisoner had the two eyes, the centered nose, the properly shaped mouth which were common to the men of Erb. Hair grew on his head, black and thick and there was a faint shadow of beard on his jaw line.

"This is a man—" her thought reached Lur.

"Why not? Did you expect a serpent? It is a pity he is dead—"

Varta felt a rich warm tide rising in her throat to answer that teasing half question. There were times when Lur's thought reading was annoying, He had risen to his hind legs so that he too could look into the shell which held their find.

"Yes, a pity," he repeated. "But—"

A vision of the turbi flowers swept through her mind. Had Lur suggested it, or had that wild thought been hers alone? Only this ship was so old—so very old!

Lur's red tongue flicked. "It can do no harm to try—" he suggested slyly and set his claws into the hoop holding the captive's right wrist, testing its strength.

"But the metal on the shore, it crumpled into powder at my touch—" she protested. "What if we carry him out only to have—to have—" Her mind shuddered away from the picture which followed.

"Did the turbi blossom fade when pulled out?" countered Lur. "There is a secret to these fastenings—" He pulled and pried impatiently.

Varta tried to help but even their united strength was useless against the force which held the loops in place. Breathless the girl slumped back against the wall of the cabin while Lur settled down on his haunches. One of the odd patches of color drifted by, its vivid scarlet like a jewel spiraling lazily upward. Varta's eyes followed its drift and so were guided to what she had forgotten, the worlds of Asti.

"Asti!"

Lur was looking up too.

"The power of Asti!"

Varta's hand went up, rested for a long moment under the sun and then drew it down, carefully, slowly, as she had in Memphir's temple. Then she stepped towards the captive. Within her hood a beaded line of moisture outlined her lips, a pulse thundered on her temple. This was a fearsome thing to try.

She held the sun on a line with one of the wrist bonds, She must avoid the flesh it imprisoned, for Asti's power could kill.

From the sun there shot an orange-red beam to strike full upon the metal. A thin line of red crept across the smooth hoop, crept and widened. Varta raised her hand, sending the sun spinning up and Lur's claws pulled on the metal. It broke like rotten wood in his grasp.

The girl gave a little gasp of half-terrified delight. Then the old legends were true! As Asti's priestess she controlled powers too great to guess. Swiftly she loosed the other hoops and restored the sun and worlds to their place over her head as the captive slumped across the threshold of his cell.

Tugging and straining they brought him out of the broken ship into the sunlight of Erb. Varta threw back her hood and breathed deeply of the air which was not manufactured by the wizardry of the lizard skin and Lur sat panting, his nostril flaps open. It was he who spied the spring on the mountain side above, a spring of water uncontaminated by the strange life of the lake. They both dragged themselves there to drink deeply.

Varta returned to the lake shore reluctantly. Within her heart she believed that the man they had brought from the ship was truly dead. Lur might hold out the promise of the flowers, but this was a man and he had lain in the water for countless ages—

So she went with lagging steps, to find Lur busy. He had solved the mystery of the space suit and had stripped it from the unknown. Now his clawed paw rested lightly on the bared chest and he turned to Varta eagerly.

"There is life—"

Hardly daring to believe that, she dropped down beside Lur and touched their prize. Lur was right, the flesh was warm and she had caught the faint rhythm of shallow breath. Half remembering old tales, she put her hands on the arch of the lower ribs and began to aid that rhythm. The breaths were deeper—

Then the man half turned, his arm moved. Varta and Lur drew back. For the first time the girl probed gently the sleeping mind before her—even as she had read the minds of those few of Memphir who had ascended to the temple precincts in the last days.

Much of what she read now was confused or so alien to Erb that it had no meaning for her. But she saw a great city plunged into flaming death in an instant and felt the horror and remorse of the man at her feet because of his own part in that act, the horror and remorse which had led him to open rebellion and so to his imprisonment. There was a last dark and frightening memory of a door closing on light and hope—

The space man moaned softly and hunched his shoulders as if he struggled vainly to tear loose from bonds.

"He thinks that he is still prisoner," observed Lur. "For him life begins at the very point it ended—even as it did for the turbi flowers. See—now he awakens."

The eyelids rose slowly, as if the man hated to see what he must look upon. Then, as he sighted Varta and Lur, his eyes went wide. He pulled himself up and looked dazedly around, striking out wildly with his fists. Catching sight of the clumsy suit Lur had taken from him he pulled at it, looking at the two before him as if he feared some attack.

Varta turned to Lur for help. She might read minds and use the wordless speech of Lur. But his people knew the art of such communication long before the first priest of Asti had stumbled upon their secret. Let Lur now quiet this outlander.

Delicately Lur sought a way into the other's mind, twisting down paths of thought strange to him. Even Varta could not follow the subtile waves sent forth in the quick examination and reconnoitering, nor could she understand all of the conversation which resulted. For the man from the ancient ship answered in speech aloud, sharp harsh sounds of no meaning. It was only after repeated instruction from Lur that he began to frame his messages in his mind, clumsily and disconnectedly.

Pictures of another world, another solar system, began to grow more clear as the space man became more at home in the new way of communication. He was one of a race who had come to Erb from beyond the stars and discovered it a world without human life: So they had established colonies and built great cities—far different from Memphir—and had lived in peace for centuries of their own time.

Then on the faraway planet of their birth there had begun a great war, a war which brought flaming death to all that world. The survivors of a last battle in outer space had fled to the colonies on Erb. But among this handful were men driven mad by the death of their world, and these had blasted the cities of Erb, saying that their kind must be wiped out.

The man they had rescued had turned against one such maddened leader and had been imprisoned just before an attack upon the largest of the colony's cities. After that he remembered nothing.

Varta stopped trying to follow the conversation—Lur was only explaining now how they had found the space man and brought him out of the wrecked ship. No human on Erb, this one had said, and yet were there not her own people, the ones who had built Memphir? And what of the barbarians, who, ruthless and cruel as they seemed by the standards of Memphir, were indeed men? Whence had they come then, the men of Memphir and the ancestors of the barbarian hordes? Her hands touched the scaled skin of the suit she still wore and then rubbed across her own smooth flesh. Could one have come from the other, was she of the blood and heritage of Lur?

"Not so!" Lur's mind, as quick as his flickering tongue, had caught that panic-born thought. "You are of the blood of this space wanderer. Men from the riven colonies must have escaped to safety. Look at this man, is he not like the men of Memphir—as they were in the olden days of the city's greatness?"

The stranger was tall, taller than the men of Memphir and there was a certain hardness about him which those city dwellers in ease had never displayed. But Lur must be right, this was a man of her race. She smiled in sudden relief and he answered that smile. Lur's soft laughter rang in both their heads.

"Asti in His Infinite Wisdom can see through Centuries. Memphir has fallen because of its softness and the evildoing of its people and the barbarians will now have their way with the lands of the north. But to me it appears that Asti is not yet done with the pattern He was weaving there. To each of you He granted a second life. Do not disdain the Gifts of Asti, Daughter of Erb!"

Again Varta felt the warm tide of blood rise in her cheeks. But she no longer smiled. Instead she regarded the outlander speculatively.

Not even a Maiden of the Temple could withstand the commands of the All Highest. Gifts from the Hand of Asti dared not be thrown away.

Above the puzzlement of the stranger she heard the chuckling of Lur.

THE END

118

www.ingramcontent.com/pod-product-compliance
Lightning Source LLC
Chambersburg PA
CBHW012025110726
47995CB00005B/1136